The Cabin
and other stories

by
James R. Coggins

Mill Lake Books

Published by Mill Lake Books
Chilliwack, BC
Canada
jamescoggins.wordpress.com/mill-lake-books

ISBN: 978-1-998787-12-8

Other books by James R. Coggins

John Smyth Mysteries
Who's Grace?
Desolation Highway
Mountaintop Drive
Springtime in Winnipeg

Other Fiction
1995: Je me souviens
Too Many Deaths
(three stories, including a John Smyth mystery)

Nonfiction
John Smyth's Congregation: English Separatism, Mennonite Influence and the Elect Nation
Living for God in a Pagan Society: What Daniel Can Teach Us

Table of Contents

The Cabin

Eloise stared at me in disbelief. "What did you say?"

"I said we should invite old John to dinner one of these Sundays."

"Who? The old guy who comes to church sometimes?"

"Yes. He seems like he could use a friend."

"But you're only an elder," my wife reminded me. "Wouldn't it be better if the pastor invited him?"

"Well, sure," I answered, "but can you see Pastor Paul inviting him home to his house with all the kids? Old John would probably feel out of place in a house full of young kids, and it might be harder for Pastor Paul to talk to him at any depth. We knew that was one of the disadvantages of hiring a young pastor like Paul."

"We wouldn't have to invite him into our house, would we?" Eloise asked.

"Oh no, no. We would just take him for lunch at a restaurant," I assured her.

"Just us and him?" she asked. "Could we invite someone else at the same time?"

"Who?" I responded. "The only other single retired man in the congregation is Trevor Williams. He's a retired university professor. He and old John wouldn't have anything in common. And we certainly can't invite any of the widow ladies."

"Certainly not," Eloise agreed.

*****

And that was how our journey with old John began.

John had been coming to Happy Valley Church, our congregation of a couple of hundred people, for a few months. He just showed up out of the blue one Sunday. He was a tall, thin man with a somewhat bushy white beard and a more pronounced bald head. He wore just an ordinary shirt and pants and an old windbreaker. He sat quietly in one of the back pews. I noticed he pulled a small, dog-eared Bible out of his coat pocket. It looked like an old one somebody had given him sometime. I suspected he just left it in that coat pocket between Sundays.

Old John seemed to be one of those people who attend church sporadically. He would sometimes be there two or three Sundays in a row, and then maybe we wouldn't see him for a month. He never gave any personal information about himself, although there was a form for that purpose put in the Sunday bulletin each week and in slots on the backs of the pews. We didn't know where he lived or what his phone number was or how old he was, although he seemed to be past retirement age. He wasn't crippled or anything, but he didn't bounce up the church steps either. When anyone talked to him, he answered slowly and quietly and didn't say very much. We really knew very little about him. He had been coming to church off and on for several months when I suggested to Eloise that we invite him to lunch.

He wasn't in church the next Sunday, but the week after that he was sitting quietly in a back pew. It was a warm, sunny, early summer day.

After the service, I made sure I got out to the church lobby before old John could leave. Catching up to him near the door, I reached out my hand and said, "John, I'm Herb Kinnear. I am one of the elders here. I wonder if you would like to have lunch with me and my wife, Eloise."

Old John took my hand. He had a firm but gentle grip. He took some time to answer, looking me in the eye for a few moments before he said slowly, "I would like that very much."

"Great," I said. "Eloise and I will be ready to go in a few minutes. We're going to take you to Mary and Martha's. It's a good family restaurant here in town, with good homestyle cooking." I didn't say it, but old John looked like he could use a good meal. We didn't want to take him anywhere too fancy where he wouldn't feel comfortable.

Old John waited quietly off to one side of the church lobby while we talked with a few of the other church people. We offered to drive John, but he said he would just follow us in his truck. He pointed out an old pick-up. Well, it was maybe not so old. It was still in reasonably good shape but looked more dirty than shiny. We drove slowly down the main street to Mary and Martha's, so he could keep up in his truck.

When we had ordered our lunch—John using that same slow, deliberate way of talking—I asked him how he had liked the sermon that morning. He said rather noncommittally that it had been a good sermon, a comment that didn't really do it justice, since Pastor Paul is a good preacher. That week's sermon had been a particularly good one, from Acts chapter 3, on Peter and John healing a lame man at the gate of the Temple.

"I thought that was particularly insightful when Pastor Paul said that people seem to know instinctively that the place of worship, the church, is the place to go to find healing," I said. I wanted to make the point because it seemed to me that old John might be someone in need of healing, emotional and spiritual if not physical, and that that was why he had started showing up at the door of our church. I thought it significant that he chose to sit in the back row of the church, just as the lame man had sat near the gate of the temple.

Old John seemed to think about what I had said for a few moments, which I took to be a good sign. Then, in that slow way of talking, he said, "But the passage says quite clearly that he was there because he expected charity, that he may have thought people going in to worship might be more generous in giving him money. It does not seem at all that he expected to be healed."

Old John paused. "The thing that has always struck me about that lame man," he said after a bit, "is that he may have sat at the gate of the temple begging for forty years and never once have gone inside. The reason is that he might not have been allowed inside. Leviticus 21 said that priests who were lame were not allowed to go near the altar to offer sacrifices, and Deuteronomy 15 said that animals which were lame could not be offered as sacrifices. As well, Second Samuel 5 reports a saying that the lame were not allowed into David's palace. None of these passages actually says that lame people could not go into the temple courts, but by the time of the New Testament, it is likely that the Jewish religious leaders would not allow the lame into even the outer courts of the temple. So, when he was healed, it is no wonder that the man ran into the temple courts to praise God because that was a privilege he had never been granted before."

He paused again, and concluded, "If there is a lesson for the church, it seems to me that it might be that the church should ponder why it still doesn't welcome broken people into the church."

I didn't know what to say to that. Not only had he missed the point of the sermon, but he seemed to be criticizing our church for not being very welcoming—when here I was taking him to lunch.

The waitress came to bring coffee then, and when she was finished, I decided to bring the conversation back to John. I asked him if he had lived in our area long, because, as I said, he had only been coming to church for a few months.

He answered that he had only moved to the area a few months back, and then he asked how long I had been coming and how long Eloise had been coming, how we had met and did we have any children. Every time I answered a question, he quickly posed another one, and the result was that through the whole meal I never managed to move the conversation back to talking about him.

When the meal was over, old John thanked me for his meal and said he had enjoyed our time together very much.

That was the first of our lunches. A few weeks later, Eloise and I invited him to lunch again. In fact, we invited him several times. Each meal went pretty much the same way—we went to Mary and Martha's, he ordered politely, he ate slowly but seemed to enjoy his food, and somehow he always seemed to keep the conversation focused on us, on our church, and on our community. I'm sure the information we provided was helpful, but I still had learned very little about the man.

Old John continued to attend church sporadically. He would be there some Sundays and not others. His commitment to Christian faith, if he had any, seemed lukewarm at best.

Then one Sunday, when we invited him to lunch, he said that he was sorry but there was somewhere he had to go that day right after church and that in fact he would not be there the next Sunday either. But then he added, "I'll tell you what. Why don't I invite you to lunch? Two weeks from today, would you come to my place for lunch?"

I was taken completely off guard. First off, I didn't know what he meant by "my place." By that, did he mean he had a favorite restaurant? And could he afford to pay for our meals, or did he expect us to pay there as well?

Since he had accepted our invitations, it seemed impolite to decline his. To gain time, I asked, "Are you sure?"

"Absolutely," he answered. "Let's do it two weeks from today. I'm looking forward to it."

When she heard about it, Eloise was even more perturbed than I was. But she didn't know how to get out of it without offending him any more than I did.

As he had said, old John was not at church the next week, but the following week he was back in his usual place. After the service, he found me in the lobby and said, "Good morning, Herb. Are we still on for lunch? Let me know when you are ready to go."

Eloise and I talked to more people than usual that morning—since I am an elder, it is part of our duty—but eventually we met up with John again and walked out of the church together.

"Uh, John, where are we going?" I asked.

"To my place," he said. "I'll drive slowly, and you can follow me in your car." Then he abruptly got into his old truck and started the engine.

As we drove, Eloise and I pondered where John might live and where he might be taking us. He still hadn't given the church his address or phone number. We didn't know if he even had a phone.

"He probably lives in one of those small apartments above the older stores along Main Street," Eloise suggested.

It sounded reasonable to me.

But we followed old John all the way down Main Street past all of the stores. And then he headed out of town, along the old coastal highway. He drove slowly and methodically, the same way he talked.

About fifteen miles out of town, the old truck slowed, and John turned left into a narrow lane between some trees. The lane twisted up a gentle slope through the trees and came out into a clearing on the edge of a high bluff looking out over the ocean. In the clearing was a small log cabin, about thirty feet long, but the shake roof extended to the left to provide cover over a space big enough to hold a couple of cars. John pulled his pick-up into one of the spaces, and we parked behind him.

It was certainly not a very impressive structure, but still it was more than we had expected.

"Did you have any trouble keeping up?" John asked as he came over to our car.

"No, of course not," I answered.

"Good. I had noticed that you always seemed to drive slowly," he said. Then he added, "Why don't you walk around out here a bit while I get lunch started. It should only take about fifteen minutes or so."

With that, he turned, unlocked the front door of the cabin, and went inside.

It was a pleasant, sunny fall afternoon, so Eloise and I did as he suggested. There was a path that ran along the edge of the cliff, next to a rough stone wall about chest high. The path offered magnificent views of the ocean to the west.

After following the path a couple of hundred feet, we came to a split rail fence. The path and the wall continued, but, fearful of trespassing on someone else's property, we turned and walked in the opposite direction. A couple of hundred feet in that direction, we came to a similar fence, so we stopped and just admired the ocean view. We could see and hear the waves crashing on the rocks far below us.

After a few minutes, we headed to the cabin and knocked on the front door. Old John opened it—I noticed it had been locked—and ushered us inside. The front half of the cabin was one long room, with a rough wooden table and some chairs to the right and a couple of couches and an easy chair grouped around a coffee table to the left. In the center of the room against the back wall was an old wood stove, with a large pot and an old metal coffee pot sitting on it. To the right of it was a kitchen alcove and then a small room along the outside wall John said was the bathroom. While Eloise went to wash up (and, if I know her, check the medicine cabinet), I wandered in the other direction. Near the outside wall to the left was a door leading to a bedroom, simply furnished, with a further door, leading to what I presumed to be a big closet at the far end of the bedroom, toward the center of the house. The floors were wood, with some throw rugs, and sunshine was pouring in through the front and side windows. It was a simple house simply furnished, providing the basic necessities. Still, it was more than I had expected.

When I turned around, I saw John pulling a tray of buns out of the stove's oven. He placed the buns in the center of the table, then ladled something from the large pot into bowls and placed one on the table in front of each chair. He then poured coffee from the coffee pot into cups. When I reached the table, I saw that the bowls were filled with a thick beef stew.

John invited us to sit and said a very simple prayer of thanks. The stew was delicious, and the buns were warm from the oven. It was a very simple meal but good and nourishing.

"John," I said, "you have a very nice little house here."

"Thank you," he answered. "This whole section of the coast, a few hundred acres, was owned for many years by the government. The idea had been to use it to keep a watch on naval traffic going up the coast. Of course, that is all done by satellite tracking now, and the government hasn't used this land for years. It's pretty far from town, and nobody seemed very interested in it."

It was about the most I had ever heard John say at any one time. The cabin seemed relatively new, and John struck me as someone who probably worked with his hands. "Did you build this cabin yourself, John?" I asked.

John smiled. "Well, no," he said. "I had some help."

I wondered who had helped him, but before I could ask anything else, John asked Eloise a question. Somehow, the conversation never got back to him, and we didn't learn any more.

Before we left, I asked John if he would mind giving me his address and phone number for the church records. He hesitated, then gave that little half-smile of his, and nodded. He didn't have any paper handy in that little cabin, so I got a church bulletin out of my Bible in the car, and he wrote on that. "John Morrison," he wrote, and it was then that I realized I had never known his last name before. He gave his address as a post office box in town, and when he wrote the phone number down, he said that he was away sometimes and he didn't always answer the phone anyway, so if I phoned and didn't get any answer, I shouldn't worry. I suspected he might go off hunting or fishing, but somehow the conversation shifted again, and I didn't ask.

As we were driving away, Eloise asked, "Did you notice anything peculiar about that cabin?"

"No," I said. "What did you notice?"

"There are spectacular views of the ocean from that spot, there are big windows on the front and sides of the cabin, but there are no windows in the back facing the ocean."

I had not noticed, but it was indeed odd. "Well," I said, "some people just have more vision than others. Maybe John doesn't care about the view."

We had had a pleasant time, but something had been bothering me, so, a couple of weeks later, we asked John out to lunch at Mary and Martha's again. I wasn't sure how to approach the question, but toward the end of the meal I made up my mind to just ask him outright.

"John, how did you come to build your cabin on that piece of government land?" I asked. "Did you have trouble getting permission?"

A look of concern or anxiety came over John's face at that point, but in a few moments the look dissipated. "Am I squatting there? Is that what you think?" he asked.

That was what I had been wondering, but I didn't want to admit that to him. "No, no," I said. "I just wondered how you got permission. Are you leasing the land? Do you have to pay rent? How did you even find out it was available?"

"No," John said. "I bought it." Then, perhaps seeing my reaction, he added, "Don't be so surprised. As I said, the government hadn't used the land for a long time, it's pretty far out of town, and nobody was interested in buying it. So, I asked if I could buy some of it, and I got it really cheap."

I wasn't sure if I believed John, but I let it go. If he didn't have a right to the land, then checking into it might only create problems for him.

*****

We had now had a few meals with John, and Christmas was approaching. One day, Eloise asked me, "Is John on the list to receive a Christmas hamper from the church this year?"

It was a good question. "I don't know," I said. "I'll have to check. Do you think he needs it? He certainly seems thin enough."

"Do you remember when we went to his cabin for lunch?" she answered. "He wouldn't let us help him clean up.

But I thought he wouldn't mind if I put the coffee cream back in the refrigerator. But when I did, I saw it was empty. There was almost nothing else in there."

"That settles it," I said. "We will bring him a Christmas hamper."

It was a rainy Saturday afternoon when we drove back out to John's place. We had a little trouble finding the laneway. It was very narrow, just a gap in the trees, and his cabin wasn't visible from the highway. But John's old truck was in its usual spot next to the cabin, so we assumed he must be home. I carried the hamper over to the front door and was about to knock when I noticed that there was a doorbell beside the door. It seemed unnecessary in such a small cabin, but I was curious about whether it was actually connected. When I pushed it, it worked, I thought. There was a faint ringing, and in a moment I could hear John calling through the door, "Who is it?" His voice sounded hollow and far away as if he was in the back bedroom.

"It's Herb, from the church," I shouted back.

"Give me a minute. I'll be right there," he said.

Then, I could hear a faint humming or whirring that seemed to be coming from inside the cabin. In a few moments, the door was unlocked, and John opened it. He was dressed in his usual plain shirt and pants.

"Hi, John," I said. "We've come to wish you a merry Christmas—and to bring you a Christmas hamper from the church." I held it up for him to see.

"But I..." he started, then stepped back, allowing me to enter.

As I put the hamper down on his table, he said, "I don't really need..."

"Nonsense, John," I said. "It's a gift. We all need help sometimes. You need to eat."

He seemed perplexed. Then, he smiled. "Herb," he said, "I am very grateful for your thoughtfulness. But do you think the church would mind if I shared some of this food with a family who live down the road a bit?"

"Well," I said, "I suppose not if that family really needs it. But you need the food too, and the food was intended for you. I don't want you to go hungry."

"Thank you very much, Herb," he said. "I will share some of the food. But don't worry about me. If I need food, I know where the food bank is, and I can go there."

And that is how we left it.

*****

We didn't see a lot of John around the church for the next few weeks, but then one Sunday he was there again. Eloise and I thought we had better take advantage of his appearance and invited him to lunch again. He seemed genuinely grateful this time, and again we had an enjoyable time. I told John we had missed him at church, a gentle hint that he should attend more regularly. But John replied that he had been away for a few weeks. He didn't say where.

This led me to ask, "You said you were not from this area. Can I ask why you moved here?"

I didn't think John was going to answer, but, after a pause, he said, "I was looking for a place to get away, a peaceful place where no one would bother me. After looking around a bit, I moved here."

I didn't quite know what to say to that, so I said nothing. For a fleeting moment, I wondered if old John was hiding out from the police or at least from bill collectors.

*****

Things continued that way for some months. John was at church maybe half the Sundays. He was always polite, but he never seemed to let anyone get very close to him.

About Easter time, a new family showed up at church—a single mother and three young boys. Pastor Paul phoned me a couple of weeks later and asked me if I had met Andrea Long. I hadn't, but Paul explained that she was the new woman. I had seen Paul and his wife, Amber, talking with her.

"Sure, sure," I said. "What about her?"

"Well, she just started coming to church at Easter. There were some other new people there also that Sunday who had come because of the Easter leaflets we had distributed in the neighborhood. But when I asked her, she said she had come partly because of the hamper the church had dropped off at Christmas."

That all sounded good to me, and I wasn't sure what Paul was getting at. "So?" I asked.

"So, I checked our list, and we don't have any record of delivering a hamper to her. In fact, we had never even heard of her before Easter."

"So, who delivered the hamper? Could it have been another church?"

"That's what I wondered, so I asked her. She said a man named John had delivered the hamper and said very clearly that it was from our church. In fact, she still had the pamphlet talking about Happy Valley Church that we had included in our hampers. She couldn't remember John's last name, she wasn't even sure she ever knew it, but she said this John had been helping her in other ways and had been talking to her about Jesus and the Bible and the church."

"That sounds good," I said, "but why are you asking me about it? How many men named John are members of the church?"

"There's four," Paul said, "but none of them is old enough to be the man Andrea described, and they all told me they know nothing about Andrea."

"So, who delivered the hamper?"

"That's what I'm hoping you can tell me," Paul said. "Didn't you deliver a Christmas hamper to old John?"

I was finally starting to see what Paul was getting at. "Old John? Yes, I did," I said. "Where does Andrea live?"

"She lives in a house trailer on a piece of property on the old coastal highway about twenty miles out of town."

"That must be it, then," I said. "Old John told me he might share some of his hamper with someone else, but he didn't say who. He must have given some to Andrea."

"It sounds more like he gave her the whole hamper," Paul said.

"That's ridiculous," I said. "Old John needed the food. He couldn't have given it all away."

Or had he? I wondered.

I still had the phone number John had given me, so I phoned him up. I was surprised when he answered on the sixth ring. Two other times over the last few months, I had called the number and got no answer.

"John, it's Herb, from the church," I said.

"Oh hello, Herb," he answered. "How are you?"

"I'm fine, John." Now that it came to it, I wasn't sure how to approach him. I hesitated, then decided to just ask him outright. "John, when we brought you the Christmas hamper last year, you said you were going to give some of the food to someone else who needed it. Did you give some food to a woman named Andrea Long?"

There was silence on the other end of the line for a few moments, then John answered, "Yes, Herb. I gave some of the food to Andrea. How did you know?"

"Well, Andrea has been coming to church the last couple of weeks, and she said—"

"Andrea has been coming to church?" John interrupted. "That's great!"

"Uh, yes," I said. "Andrea has been coming to church. She said you had been talking to her about Jesus and the church."

"Well, I did what I could," John countered. "I did say Happy Valley was a good church and I thought she would like it there. I said that maybe the church could help her like it helped me."

"Speaking of that, John," I said, "how much food did you give Andrea? Did you give her the whole hamper?"

"Not all of it," he admitted, "but a lot of it. Her boyfriend left her and the kids some time ago, and she really needed it. And it did help convince her to go to church."

"That's all great, John," I said. "Happy Valley Church is glad to help Andrea too. But that food was intended for you."

"I appreciate that, Herb," John answered. "But my wants are simple. I don't need much. And, like I said, if I ever need food, I go to the food bank."

*****

I left it at that. And I didn't leave it. It concerned me. A week later, I phoned Steve Archibald, director of the local food bank and asked him if he knew an older man named John Morrison.

"Yes, he's been here several times," Steve answered, somewhat cautiously I thought.

"Did you give him food?"

Steve didn't answer for a few moments. "Mr. Morrison asked me to keep the nature of his involvement with the food bank confidential," he said finally.

"Come on, Steve. You consult with the churches all the time to coordinate our caring ministries."

"I can't in this case. Mr. Morrison asked me to keep his involvement confidential, and I have agreed."

"Can't you at least tell me if you have ever given him any food?"

Again, there was a long pause. "Well, okay. I have on occasion given some food to Mr. Morrison."

"Thanks, Steve. That's all I wanted to know."

But was it?

*****

A few weeks later, another man started showing up at church. He was tall and thin with a few days' growth of beard and stained blue jeans. He looked pretty rough around the edges and, if possible, spoke even less than old

John. He reminded me of old John in some other ways too. He was a loner like John, but much younger, probably in his late twenties. I suppose my experience with old John had made it easier for me to approach someone like him, so, I introduced myself. He said his name was Billy Markoff, and I asked him if he would like to join Eloise and me for lunch.

He hesitated, then nodded and said, "Thanks."

Old John was standing nearby, and, on an impulse, I went over and asked him if he would like to join us too. He gave me a rather odd smile and said he would be delighted, one of the most enthusiastic responses I had ever had from him.

When we were ready to leave, I asked Billy if he had a car or if he would like to ride with us. He accepted the ride, while John traveled separately, in his old pick-up truck.

When we reached Mary and Martha's restaurant, I was about to introduce the two men, but before I could do so, Billy said, "Hi, John."

"You two know each other?" I asked.

A look passed between them, and Billy became silent. John said, "Billy lives out on the highway near my place. Remember I told you that I had help building my cabin? Billy helped me with that and with some other things around my place."

As I said, Billy seemed to talk even less than old John, but I did find out that Billy was a trained carpenter, but he didn't seem to have a full-time job, just got by doing odd jobs. I began to suspect there might be some underlying problems, but old John seemed to change the subject whenever I asked Billy anything personal.

It was an enjoyable meal nevertheless, with old John talking about the birds and small animals he saw out in the woods, and Billy joining in.

After the meal, I offered to drive Billy home, but John said he could take him since he lived out that way.

Billy came to church pretty regularly after that, sometimes coming with old John and sometimes just seeming to show up without me seeing how he got there. In time, he started to dress a little better, in newer, cleaner blue jeans.

A month or so later, another new family showed up at church, Jude and Alicia Mancini and their two children. Since they were younger, Pastor Paul and his wife Amber invited them to their place for lunch.

But Pastor Paul phoned me later that week with a question. "It's the new couple, Jude and Alicia Mancini," he said. "They told me they found out about Happy Valley Church through the highway Bible study group."

"What highway Bible study group?" I asked.

"Precisely," he answered. "Apparently, they are attending a Bible study at Mark and Sue Collins' house."

I knew the couple he meant. Mark and Sue had started coming to the church a year or two earlier. Mark was a school teacher and Sue a nurse, and they had a couple of teenagers, who were involved in our youth group. Other than that, I didn't know much about them. They hadn't been very active in the church, as far as I knew. If there was a Bible study at their house, it certainly wasn't one of the Bible studies officially connected to the church.

"Did you ask Mark and Sue about it?" I asked.

"Yes," Pastor Paul answered. "Apparently, they do have a weekly Bible study at their place. I asked if they would like to make it one of the official church Bible studies, but they politely declined. Mark doesn't mind talking to me about the group from time to time, but he said he was afraid some of the people coming might not come if it was officially connected to a church."

"Did he say who those people were?"

"No. I gather that they mostly live out along the coastal highway near Mark and Sue's place, but he didn't give me any names."

That didn't surprise me. People who lived out along the highway often chose to live there because they wanted to be left alone. Even though it was not that far from town, the highway didn't lead anywhere, ending about forty or fifty miles up the coast, and the area was quite desolate.

We left it at that, but it made me curious. About a week later, I phoned Mark up. I told him that, as an elder of the church, I wanted to commend him for starting a Bible study with his neighbors in that area. I told Mark I would respect his wish not to give out names, but I asked if he could tell me if old John ever came to the study. It may have been my imagination, but it seemed that Mark became hesitant before answering guardedly, "He comes sometimes."

That didn't surprise me. Old John showed an interest in the Christian faith, but he wasn't any more consistent or committed to the Bible study than he was to our church.

*****

In late summer, old John surprised Eloise and me by inviting us to his place again for lunch. It was a beautiful day, and again we walked in the woods along the coast while John made dinner. He had prepared stew, buns, and coffee again, and I began to wonder if he knew how to cook anything else. I didn't think very hard about what kind of meat might be in the stew, remembering John's conversation about the small birds and animals he saw in the woods.

"This is a great little place you have here, John," I said. "How is it again you came to settle here?"

His face seemed to light up then, almost as if he welcomed the question. But he was silent for a while before answering. "I find it peaceful and quiet here," he said. "My wife died a couple of years ago, and I needed a place to get away and heal."

I was stunned. It was the most personal information John had ever shared about himself. I had always figured John for a loner and had never suspected that he might have been married. I asked Eloise about it later, and she was as surprised as I was. She pointed out that we had never seen so much as a photograph in that sterile little cabin of his.

Trying to keep the conversation going, I said, "John, I'm very sorry. How did she die?"

23

I don't know what I was expecting. The idea briefly flitted through my head that maybe he had killed his wife and was hiding from the police.

But he answered with a single word: "Cancer."

I wanted to know more, but apparently old John had said all he was intending to say. Afterward, I wondered if he might have invited us there just so he could tell us that little bit of information. Maybe he could only reveal himself in small doses. Before we could ask anything else, somehow the conversation shifted. John said something about the food and asked a question, and we got no more details about his private life.

This time, old John let Eloise and me help clear the dishes off the table. In the process, Eloise got a quick look into the cupboards and refrigerator and reported later to me that there was more food there than there had been on our previous visit.

*****

It was about two weeks later. The church service had just started, and I was on the platform giving some announcements when old John walked into the back of the church with an attractive, red-headed woman I judged to be in her late thirties. I was so surprised, I lost track of what I was saying. A number of people in the congregation turned to see what I was looking at. Old John and the woman slid into one of the back pews, followed by a tall, middle-aged man about old John's height but not as thin, and two red-haired girls about eight or ten.

After the service, John approached me with a look on his face that was both shy and a little sheepish. "I'm sorry I interrupted the announcements," he said. "Herb, this is my son Dylan, my daughter-in-law Roxanne, and my granddaughters Faith and Hope."

Dylan reached out and shook my hand. I could see the resemblance to his father. "It's a pleasure to meet you, Mr.

Kinnear," he said. "My father has told me so much about you and your church."

Apparently a lot more than he had told us about his family.

I invited old John and his family to join us for lunch, but John said he had prepared lunch back at his cabin for the family.

I did manage to learn that Dylan worked for a big construction company, that he and his family had flown in to spend the last week of summer with old John, and that they would be leaving in a few days. With his construction experience, I wondered if Dylan had helped old John build his cabin.

I asked them where they were staying while they were visiting, but John interrupted. "In the cabin," he said.

I must have looked shocked because Dylan reassured me: "Don't worry. There is plenty of room." And he smiled.

I doubted his words, but I couldn't say that openly.

After they had left, I asked Eloise, "Do you think that old John might have known a couple of weeks ago that his family was coming? Maybe he invited us to his cabin on purpose to tell us he had been married, so we wouldn't be so surprised when they showed up."

"I doubt it," she said. "But with old John just about anything is possible."

*****

After that, things continued on again without much change. Old John continued to show up at church intermittently. We were invited to the cabin one more time that year and found everything there much as it had been, except that there was now a photo of Dylan and his family on a side table. John served stew and buns again.

But if things remained the same with old John, elsewhere things were changing quickly. Mark and Sue Collins seemed to be doing remarkable things. Over the next three years, more than a dozen other people showed up at church, claiming to have either become Christians or to have found out about the church through the highway Bible study held at their place.

I don't remember when it was that I found out that both Billy Markoff and Andrea Long were attending the Bible study along the highway, but the next summer both of them were baptized as Christian believers in Happy Valley Church. About eight months after that, Pastor Paul announced that Billy and Andrea were getting married and everyone in the church was invited to the wedding. I never did find out where Billy had been living, but after the wedding, he moved into Andrea's trailer. I happened to go by it some time later and noticed that the yard had been cleaned up, the trailer had been painted, and an addition had been built onto the back, doubling the size of the house. A year later, Andrea delivered a baby boy she named William John.

Dylan and his family came back to visit old John for a week every summer. "The girls really love staying in Grandpa's cabin," Dylan told me. I suppose for them it would be something like camping out, although I couldn't imagine sleeping on the wood floor of the cabin could have been all that comfortable.

Old John and Dylan politely but firmly, perhaps even a bit reluctantly it seemed, resisted all of my invitations to lunch. However, on the third visit, Dylan took me quietly aside in the church lobby. "Dad is getting older, you know. If anything ever happens to him, I would appreciate you getting in touch with me right away."

I readily agreed, of course. It was hard to judge old John's age. He still seemed relatively healthy, and he didn't seem to be losing his faculties. On the other hand, it was true that he seemed frailer than he had when I had first met him. "I would be glad to do that, Dylan," I said, "but John, well, he doesn't come to church every Sunday, and if anything happens to him out at the cabin, I won't know for quite a while."

Dylan waved that possibility aside. "I know. I'm not asking you to do anything extra, but I understand he has some contact with some of his neighbors, and if you do hear anything from anybody who lives out along the highway, I would appreciate you letting me know."

I assured him I would, and he gave me a business card, saying, "That's my work number, and my home number and cell phone number are written on the back."

When I looked at the card later, I discovered that he did indeed work for a construction company—as vice-president for finance.

*****

I did not have occasion to use that card until four years later. The congregation was quite a bit bigger by that time, and we had just stood up to sing the closing song. For some reason, I looked back at old John in his usual back pew. He stood up with the rest of the congregation, and then he was down. He leaned forward toward the back of the pew in front of him and then twisted sideways, landing on his back in the aisle. I rushed over immediately, and so did a number of other people. As I looked down, old John's eyes locked onto mine, and then a most peaceful look came over his face, and he was gone. There were people in the congregation who knew CPR, and we called an ambulance immediately, but old John was gone, and he was not coming back.

I dug that card out of my wallet and phoned Dylan from the hospital. "Dylan," I said when he answered, "it's Herb Kinnear. I'm sorry to have to tell you that your Dad collapsed in church this morning. We called an ambulance, of course, but there was nothing that could be done. I'm so sorry. He's gone."

There was silence for a long time, and then Dylan said in a husky voice, "In church, you said? Dad would have been glad about that."

Dylan arrived the next day. He phoned me from the airport and asked me to meet him at the cabin that afternoon.

When I got there, Dylan's rental car was parked in the second slot under the overhang, next to old John's battered pick-up. Rather than leave it in the church parking lot, I had asked one of the church members to drive that old truck back to old John's home the night before. Old John's place had always seemed a peaceful spot, but this afternoon, in spite of the bright sunshine, it seemed desolate and empty.

Dylan met me outside. We shook hands formally. Then he said, "Roxanne and the kids will be flying in tomorrow. I've been to the hospital and made arrangements. There will be a big funeral back home, but Dad had asked if there could be a memorial service in Happy Valley Church. He wanted his ashes buried here at the cabin."

"Of course," I said. "We would be glad to do anything we can." I thought that some of the people who lived out along the highway at least might like to come to the memorial service.

"I understand Dad had invited you and Eloise out to the cabin for lunch a few times?"

I nodded.

"That was a rare privilege. I suppose he served you Campbell's chunky soup and called it stew?" he said.

While I was still trying to get my head around that, Dylan asked, "Did you ever ask Dad to preach at your church?"

"Preach?" I said. "No. Why would we?"

"He never told you who he was, did he?"

"He said his name was John Morrison…"

"Yes, his name was John Morrison," Dylan answered. "That is certainly true." Then he suggested we go inside.

It seemed as desolate and empty inside the cabin as outside, as if no one had ever lived there.

Dylan shut and locked the door carefully. I was thinking we would sit down in the living room area or the kitchen, but Dylan led me through into the back bedroom and opened the double doors of the closet. There was another set of polished steel doors just inside the wooden doors. Dylan pushed a button, the doors slid open, and Dylan led me inside a small, metal-lined cubicle. The doors slid closed, he pushed another button, and the cubicle suddenly lurched downward.

The elevator stopped and opened into a long narrow room, with a hotel lobby counter in front of us. But Dylan led me to the right into another room about sixty feet long and thirty feet wide. A row of windows covered the entire sixty feet of wall, offering a magnificent view of the ocean. The room was furnished with comfortable living room furniture.

"My father told you that the military once owned this property and used it to monitor ship traffic on the ocean," Dylan said then. "I understand he also suggested to you that he was able to buy a piece of the property for his cabin. That is not entirely true. My father was able to buy the entire property, over a hundred acres. The purchase included an extensive underground facility built into the cliff facing the ocean. Those windows that you see are made of a special glass that has a very dark tint on the other side. From the ocean, all that glass looks like a rock cliff face. There was only a small building above ground—it looked like a utility shed, but it was made of reinforced concrete and held the elevator. My father had his cabin built around it, perfectly camouflaging it."

Dylan led me across the room to where a glass door led to a long hall. Doors were spaced evenly along its length. Dylan opened the first door on the right. Inside was a spacious, well-furnished bedroom, with one wall again mostly devoted to glass, offering a magnificent view of the ocean. However, in this room there were deep blue curtains, pulled back to let in the light. There were several framed photos on the walls; Dylan and his family were in some, but not in all of them.

"This was Dad's bedroom," Dylan said.

He led me to the next room on the same side, which was similar. "These were the quarters for the military staff stationed here, although the furnishings have been changed," he continued. "This is where Roxanne and I stayed when we visited. Our daughters slept in the next room. The rooms on the other side of the hall are similar, except they have no view of the ocean."

Up to this point, I had been feeling too overwhelmed to say much of anything. "Who are the other people in the photos in your Dad's room?" I asked.

"Dad's family," Dylan answered. He paused. "Did Dad tell you about Esther and David?"

I shook my head no.

"Dad and Mom had three children. I'm the youngest. Esther is the oldest. She runs an orphanage in the Philippines and is married to Ricardo, a Filipino. They have five kids. And David is principal of a Bible college in Nigeria. He and Sandra have three kids. Both families have been here, but only a couple of times, and I'm not surprised that you have never seen them at your church. It is hard for them to get away from their work. Dad went to see them more often than they came here, and when they were back home, they usually stayed with Roxanne and me, which was closer to their supporting churches."

While he was talking, Dylan had led me back across the big "living room." There was a glass door on this side too, but in this case, it led to a large room filled with tables and chairs. To our right, on the side away from the ocean view, was a long counter, and behind it an industrial-sized kitchen.

"This is the cafeteria." Dylan continued his tour. Going around the end of the counter, he walked over to a massive cooking surface. "This place was built quite ingeniously," he said. "This stove, for instance, could cook dozens of meals at a time, or you can just turn on one burner and cook a single meal. That's what Dad did. The refrigerator and freezer are similar. They are divided into sections, and you can use as many, or as few, as you need."

Coming out from behind the counter, Dylan led me across the cafeteria to a door at the other end. Behind this door were stairs, leading up and down.

"There are three underground levels in this facility," Dylan said. "Besides the outside elevator we used, there are two other interior elevators at the back. The bottom level contains more sleeping quarters for the personnel. There is a lounge, but no kitchen."

But Dylan was leading me up the stairs to the top level. I noticed that the stairs continued up. "The stairs at each end of the building lead up to fire escape hatches," he said. "And at the bottom level, they lead to paths down to the beach. There are sprinkler systems throughout the building. It meets all the fire codes."

But Dylan didn't lead me any farther up or down but through a door that led off the landing. "This is the operations level," he said, "where all the work was done. All of the equipment has been removed, and Dad has had considerable renovations done here."

There was a central hall here as well, with what looked like meeting rooms on the ocean side, again with those magnificent views. The central meeting room was as large as the "living room" on the floor above, and there were padded chairs arranged in rows that could seat two or three hundred people.

"Dad's vision was to turn this facility into a Christian retreat center after he died. The kitchen was already there, and guests can stay in the former staff quarters. This floor will be used for prayer, teaching and worship. Renovations have been going on since Dad moved in, and they are almost complete now."

Dylan opened large double doors on the land side of the facility opposite the large room and turned on a light. There were rows and rows of bookcases, interspersed with desks and tables.

"This is the theological library," Dylan said. Dad's own library forms the base for it, but some colleagues have promised to donate their libraries as well."

It all finally fell into place. "Your Dad was John Morrison, the famous theologian?"

Dylan nodded. "You had no idea?"

I shook my head. "Not a clue. Your father never showed us more than the cabin upstairs."

I was having trouble digesting everything that Dylan had told me. "John Morrison the theologian?" I asked again. "I have several of his books. I'm reading his new book *Looking Forward to Heaven* now."

I was going to add that when I had finished reading it, I had planned to pass it on to old John, thinking it might help him. But I realized then how ridiculous that would have been. I could imagine old John having a good laugh if I had done that. I thought also of John Morrison's other recent books. I ticked them off silently in my head: *Time Alone with God*, *Recovering from Death*, *Family Down the Road*, and *The Ordinary Christian*. They were all part of Morrison's The High Way series of books. That got me thinking about the highway Bible study that so many of our church's new members had been attending and wondering what curriculum they might have been studying and who had really been leading it.

Dylan interrupted my thoughts, handing me an envelope. "Dad left this for you."

The envelope was addressed, "To my friend, Herb Kinnear." I opened the envelope and pulled out a single, handwritten sheet of paper. It said:

Dear Herb,

Please forgive me for not sharing with you before this the secret of The Cabin. I was enjoying too much your attempts to help me. But it is also true that I felt it necessary to maintain a place of solitude. After my wife died, I needed a place to heal. And I needed a place to pray and think and study. I had begun to realize that I was mortal, and there were a number of books I felt I needed to get written before I died. I was also continuing my speaking ministry at retreats and conferences and in churches. It is this, not a wavering commitment to

Jesus, which explains my frequent absences from Happy Valley Church. That, and trips to visit my family. As I got older, I found those ministry trips increasingly tiring, and I needed a place to rest, away from the constant phone calls and people knocking on my door. If it had gotten out where I was living, my peace would have been disturbed.

Herb, I am very grateful for you and your church. You provided me an opportunity to be just an ordinary Christian, to be accepted as just another sinner saved by grace.

If you are reading this, I assume Dylan has told you of my plans to turn The Cabin into a retreat center. I am asking you to consider sitting on the board of the retreat center as a representative of Happy Valley Church. I hope you will accept. In setting up the center, I have included a provision that Happy Valley Church is to have use of the retreat center for retreats and other events free of charge for a period of twenty years.

I have made a similar arrangement for Steve Archibald of the food bank. I told you that I went there to get food when I needed it. That was true only to a point. I went there to get food for Andrea Long as she was then, not for me. And I did make a donation or two to the food bank from time to time.

In that context, I hope the new board will find positions for Billy and Andrea Markoff at the retreat center. Andrea has been doing housekeeping and some cooking for me over the past few years and has been very helpful. Billy is an excellent handyman, he has kept everything at The Cabin in good repair, and he has been doing many of the renovations that were needed. I hope you are not offended that I let them in on the secret of The Cabin while leaving you in the dark. It was necessary, as I needed their help, and they have little idea of my life outside. They just think of me as the eccentric man down the road.

Your friend,
Old John

Then, written in other ink at the bottom of the page were the words:

I thought then of what I had said that first time John had
invited Eloise and me to the cabin and how true it had been:
Some people have more vision than others. Some people
have the ability to see more deeply than others.

Idle Speculation and the Tree

Adam stood on the balcony of his new apartment, looking around. Before him lay a valley full of houses and stores. There was a library, a medical center, a post office, and a church. There was also a large tree rising up beside the building, not far away.

The sun shone warmly, and a light breeze stirred the branches of the tree. Idly, Adam wondered if, stepping over the railing and poising himself on the narrow ledge on the other side, he could leap out and catch the branches without plunging to the ground four floors below. "Idle speculation," he thought, but it was a Sunday morning, and with his unpacking finished, what else was there to do? What harm could come of it?

Besides, the tree might prove useful some day—as an escape route in case of fire, for instance.

Adam tried to judge the distance to the nearest branch. "About six feet," he thought. Farther, of course, past the twiggy branch ends to a limb that could support his weight, but how far? Could he leap that far?

He decided to try an experiment. Standing at one end of the balcony against the railing, he leaped toward the other end of the balcony and landed reaching forward, sprawled on his hands and knees. He marked the place where his feet had landed with the leg of a lounge chair. He stood and surveyed the distance. "Not bad," he thought, "for one who isn't an athlete." But was it far enough? He looked at the marked distance on the balcony and then across to the tree branches stretching out maybe six feet away. "How far?" he wondered.

He got out his carpenter's tape and measured his leap. Five feet, two inches, the height of a short man. Was it enough? Certainly, the tree looked farther away than that, but it was hard to tell.

There were also other factors involved. Upon landing, he had fallen forward, his hands reaching out. Surely it was his hands that mattered, not his feet. That would add at least another six feet. Or would it? Would the force of gravity suck him down into the gap between the tree and the building before he could stretch out his hands?

Also, he had fallen forward *after* his feet had landed. Would his hands be able to stretch out as far when his feet had nothing solid beneath them to push out from?

Another thing. He had been standing on solid ground when he had made his leap. Would he be able to get as good a push-off when standing on the narrow ledge beyond the railing? Perhaps not, but in the act of leaping would the adrenaline, or whatever it was that made you perform above your ability in crucial moments, not start to flow? Would he not be stronger, braver, more intense on the verge of his leap?

"And what if I missed that first branch that seems to be beckoning me out there?" he thought. Perhaps he could propel himself through the air somehow and reach another branch lower down. After all, wasn't it natural for falling things to arc out, to go farther out as they fell down? Of course, the falling would become greater all the time and the reaching out less, but wouldn't those last few inches bring him finally to the safety of the tree?

The tree. In his wondering whether he could do it, Adam had not given much thought to the tree. He had been questioning his own powers, his strength, his determination, his courage, his wisdom in calculating the best way to leap.

Regarding the tree, he had considered only how far away it was and how much brush he would have to get past before he reached solid wood.

A more difficult question was whether there was solid wood there at all. It was an old tree, gnarled and weather-beaten. Would any of its branches hold the weight of a man, or would they snap off and crumble to the ground, whichever of them he tried to grab onto? It was a question Adam had not considered before. If the tree would not hold a man anyway, all of his idle speculation was useless. The question was irrelevant, he decided. After all, he wasn't actually going to try it. He was just wondering if he could leap that far. The important thing was not the tree but Adam himself.

Adam got out his tape measure again and stretched it out toward the tree. About three feet away from the balcony, it buckled toward the ground, and the bend ran rapidly back along the tape to his hand. He drew in the rule and tried again. This time, he reached his hand out as far as he could toward the tree to hold the rule from bending. Slowly, he inched it out farther and farther toward the tree. Four feet. Four feet, six inches. Four feet, eight, nine, ten, eleven. About five feet, the tape buckled again and plunged down into the gap between the balcony and the tree until stopped by his hand.

Once more he tried. This time he stretched out his whole body toward the tree. The tape went past five feet. Five feet, six inches. Five feet, nine inches. It was getting close to the tip of the nearest branch now. Five feet, ten inches. Five feet, eleven. Six feet. Again, it buckled. He tried once more, and again it buckled. The rule failed just short of the tree. It would not reach.

"What does it matter?" he thought. I can *see* the distance. I don't have to measure it. Why do men always have to measure things? It's a leap of faith. If I could measure it, it wouldn't count. It's the man, not the distance, that matters.

Somewhat piqued, he left off his idle speculation for that Sunday morning.

However, the next Sunday morning, he again thought of the tree, the beckoning branch, the balcony, the leap...the ground if he missed.

In time, it became a habit. Not every day, not even every Sunday—he wasn't really serious about it; it did not become a duty for him—but often on a Sunday morning, *especially* on a Sunday morning, when there was nothing else to do, he would stand on the balcony, stare at the tree, and wonder if he could make the leap.

On one such morning, his mind (and eye) wandered to the people on the other balconies. Were they watching him? What would they think of him if he tried it? What would they do if he stepped over the railing and looked toward the tree, as if he were going to jump? Would they shout, "Jump! Jump!" as they do in the city and on bridges?

But it was not jumping that he contemplated. It was leaping. Not suicide, but a leap to prove he was very much alive.

More to the point, what did the people on the other balconies think of him now? Watching him standing day by day on his balcony, did they know what he was thinking? Could they guess? Were they, too, wondering if they could make the leap? Idle speculation goes to ridiculous lengths sometimes.

It must be folly then. The people on the other balconies would see it so. Would their laughter be the last thing he heard in the few fleeting seconds it would take for him to hurtle to his death? But what if he made it? Would they still say it was all folly?

Time passed, and the habit became stronger, although it was not yet anywhere near an obsession. It was a form of recreation, like regularly attending hockey games—or ballet, with its airy leaps.

Once again on a Sunday morning, Adam tested his leap along the balcony. Only four feet, eleven inches this time. He tried again. Five feet, one. He kept trying until he had raised his best leap to five feet, three and a half inches, but he was not consistent. Sometimes it was more, sometimes less.

What would it be if he really tried it? He would not be able to try it several times then. There would be only one attempt. What if it was a poor leap? He was confident that when the time came (*if* the time came, he corrected), he would be ready. It would be a good leap, a great leap, the best leap of his life—he hoped.

Still, it wouldn't hurt to practice. He leaped across the balcony again.

Periodically he began to repeat the action. At first, it was just an adjunct to his speculation, but then it, too, became a habit, and in the end, a daily ritual, preformed in the morning, a form of bodily exercise. "To keep me in shape," he thought "—just as the speculation keeps my mind sharp."

His leaps improved. Five feet, six inches. Five feet, eight. Five feet, ten and a half. Six feet, one and a quarter. "An impressive leap," he thought the morning he achieved it. But it was not a leap, and deep down he knew it. It was only a practice and not a real leap. It did not count. Idle speculation had become a serious concern—and, if it were to culminate in action, it would become a matter of life and death.

Then, one day, almost without thinking about it, he went farther. The constant preoccupation with the leap had so filled his consciousness that it seemed a natural thing to attempt it. One morning, instead of trying the leap across the balcony, he stepped over the railing, balanced on his toes on the narrow ledge beyond—and leaped out, toward the tree or ground.

His leap was short. He fell. The ground of death beckoned four floors below. Then, the tree reached out its branches and caught him.

A Visit to Edenvale

It was a long and winding road up to Edenvale Estates in the brown hills above the city, and Devon took it with some trepidation. He had no concerns about finding the house—he had been there numerous times—but he had considerable anxiety about how he would find John.

As he pulled into the driveway, he observed that the lawn and shrubs were as perfectly manicured as ever but that there appeared to be new flowers. Everything seemed greener than the last time he had been there. That had been at least a year and a half ago.

The man who opened the door was six inches shorter than Devon and twenty years older. He greeted Devon warmly. "Devon! Thank you for coming."

"Hi, John. It's good to see you. I'm sorry I didn't come sooner, but I just got back on Sunday."

"You've been on sabbatical?"

Devon nodded.

"Good trip?"

"Yes, but I didn't go as far as you did."

John smiled. He seemed tanned and healthy, not quite what Devon had expected. But the lines around his eyes had deepened—perhaps just from age, but maybe also from something else. "Did your research go well?"

"Well enough. I should be able to pull at least a couple of articles out of the research I did."

"Then your trip was more productive than mine. I won't get anything—no field notes."

"Look, John, we don't have to talk about this."

"It's okay. I want to tell someone. This is probably the most significant discovery of my career, and it will never be published. So, it helps to at least talk about it."

"John, look, I can't..."

"They told you not to talk to me, didn't they?"

"No, John, nothing like that."

"But they did talk to you, didn't they?"

Devon shrugged. "The dean and the department head just warned me not to do anything to jeopardize my career."

"Not to do anything like listen to my story or offer any support for it?"

"Something like that."

"I'm on leave. Did you know that?"

"Yes, I heard."

"Officially, it's only until I recover from my ordeal. Unofficially, it will be for five years, until I retire. They can't have professors spouting nonsense."

"Why not? It's done all the time."

John smiled. "I'll just give you an outline of my travels then, spare you the details. Let's go through to the patio. I have prepared some iced tea. I seem to prefer it outside these days. I haven't fully gotten used to being indoors yet."

When they were settled in chairs on the patio, John was silent for a few minutes and then began to speak. "You are aware that our expedition was attacked?"

"Yes, reports started reaching the university a couple of days after the first survivors stumbled out of the jungle. It was weeks before we had a clear understanding of what had happened. By then, it seemed pretty unlikely that any more survivors would be walking out on their own. The army eventually found some bodies but not all of those who were still missing. It was assumed that the rebels had either killed you or taken you captive."

"Rebels!" John snorted. "We call them rebels and guerrillas because that makes them easier to comprehend, as if they had some grand purpose, even if misguided. It's nonsense. They were just violent young men with guns and no restraint, examples of irrational human evil."

Devon smiled. "You could always apply to teach international relations instead of biology."

John ignored the comment. "You thought I was dead."

"Not at first, but after a couple of months..." Devon shrugged. "Well, by then, the consensus was pretty much that you were never coming back."

"Fortunately, my nephew didn't need my money. Before I left for my sabbatical, I had set up everything so my bills would be paid automatically. The cleaning service kept cleaning the house, and the yard service kept mowing the lawn. I wasn't even necessary in my own house."

There was an ironic edge to the older man's words that made Devon slightly uneasy. "What did happen exactly?" he asked.

"It was an area with heavy undergrowth. I don't think it was a very well planned attack. Maybe the 'rebels,' as you call them, just stumbled across us by accident and started shooting. Whatever the case, when the shooting began, we turned and ran for our lives. I headed for where the bush seemed to be the thickest. When they shot me, I kept running."

"They shot you? I didn't know that."

"Yes. One bullet went through my right shoulder, and another through the muscle in my left thigh. I had other cuts, but whether they were caused by bullets or by the bushes and rocks I don't know. I do know I was in a lot of pain and I was bleeding quite badly."

"What did you do?"

"Just collapsed eventually. By that time, I couldn't hear shooting, either because it had stopped or because I was too far away. I lost consciousness for a while. When I came around, I got up and started walking. I had no idea where I was or where I was going. I was probably in shock. When it got dark, I fell down and passed out. In the morning, I started walking again. I found a spring and then a small stream and some fruit trees. I went on that way for a long time, several days at least." John paused. "Look, did they tell you anything of what happened after that?"

"No," Devon said. "The university hasn't said very much at all. They just suggested that you had been through quite an ordeal, lost in the jungle all those months. There's been all kinds of speculation about you being held captive by tribesmen, tortured by rebels, attacked by crocodiles and snakes. It is generally conceded that the most plausible explanation is that it's all tied up in politics, that you were held captive by rebels and the university paid a big ransom to get you out, for instance. But the university isn't saying anything."

John looked thoughtful. "No, they wouldn't."

"What did happen? Can you tell me?"

John sighed. "The rebel attack is part of the public record, but the university especially does not want me to talk about what happened after that."

"What did happen? Did they pay a ransom?"

"No, nothing like that." He paused. "Look, Devon. I was in the jungle a long time. I was badly injured, in shock, possibly delirious. The university doesn't want me talking about it because they don't know how much of what I remember is real, and they are afraid if I say too much, it might discredit the university."

"I don't understand."

"I'm not sure I understand either." John paused for a long time. "Devon," he said finally, "I am going to tell you what I saw and experienced. You may not believe it. I'm not sure I believe it myself. But it's what I remember." He turned and looked solemnly at the younger man. "Devon, you must promise not to tell anyone else."

"Why?

"Because the university has told me that if I make any attempt to speak publicly about what I saw, they will take away my salary and pension benefits. The same would apply to you. It would jeopardize your career if you said anything."

"But why?"

"Come, Devon. You are an intelligent man, and you understand how universities work."

Devon thought a moment and then said, "I suppose it is because the university is committed to the scientific method, and they don't want professors expounding theories about things that cannot be observed, measured, and recorded."

"Precisely."

"Okay."

"You know me," John went on. "You know I am committed to the scientific method as well?"

"Of course."

"Then perhaps you can tell me why the university administration is so sure of what is or is not out there in the jungle when I, the only one who was there to make observations, am not sure at all what is there."

"I don't know. I can't answer that."

"Of course not," John said. "There is no answer to that. As far as the university is concerned, there are some trails we can't follow the evidence down. Nevertheless, I am going to tell you what I saw, and you must promise not to tell anyone else."

"That doesn't sound right to me."

"Just promise."

"Okay. It's your story, your research, your discovery. I promise I won't say anything."

After a moment, John picked up his narrative. "I was still badly injured and had not been eating properly. I was in a kind of stupor and probably close to death. It was early one morning, and I was thrashing blindly through the jungle when I fell. I had fallen many times, of course, but this was different. My sensation was that I was falling not just down but also back. That doesn't make sense, I know, but that was my sensation. And I was falling down. It appears I had stumbled over the side of a steep valley and rolled all the way down through the brush to the bottom.

"I came to my senses lying on the jungle floor, just as I had many times before. But this was different. I can't explain the feeling I had except to say that I felt content. This time, I did not get up and keep going. I just stayed there. Maybe I was exhausted, I had finally run out of energy, or I had reached the end of my fear. I looked around and saw that I was in a deep, lush valley. There was a stream running nearby, and I drank deeply from that. Later on, when I explored the valley more, I discovered there were four streams running through it. There were also all kinds of fruits and vegetables growing wild, randomly throughout the jungle, every kind you could think of. I ate until I was full, and every day I felt a little better. My wounds gradually healed, and after a few weeks I noticed the pain was entirely gone.

"I had no need of shelter. The temperature was always moderate, and I don't recall it ever raining. The vegetation seemed to be adequately watered by the streams and the morning dew.

"I was content to stay there, and I didn't even think about how long I had been there. Oh, it's clear looking back that it must have been well over a year, but I did not realize that then. There were days and nights, but I had no sense of time passing.

"As I explored the valley, I saw new species of insects and butterflies, at least new to me. I had no reference books to clarify whether I was discovering something new or someone else had discovered these before me. I began naming them, but I had no pen or paper to record the names and characteristics, and there were so many I eventually became confused and gave up.

"One day, I saw a remarkable sight. Coming into a clearing, I unexpectedly discovered a male lion, half hidden in the grass. Lying beside it in the long grass was what I took to be a fresh kill, a small deer or antelope. I was only about twenty feet away, and I was terrified. It is not a wise thing to interrupt a large carnivore at a fresh kill. I started backing away immediately. The lion must have been startled by my sudden appearance as well. Perhaps he had never seen a human being before, for I saw no signs of any other human being in that valley. He raised his head, and just at that moment the deer leapt to its feet and bounded away. I must have surprised the lion just in time to save the deer, for it seemed not to be hurt badly at all. In the fleeting glance I had of it, I could see no wounds. I kept backing away and was soon back among the trees. Fortunately, the lion did not follow."

John paused in his narrative. Feeling that he should say something, Devon commented, "It seems a remarkable place. I'm surprised you didn't stay longer."

"It surprises me too, looking back," John said. "I could have stayed. But one day, I just wandered away. I don't know why. I had everything I needed there, except perhaps companionship. As wonderful as that place was, I had a growing sense that it was not good for me to be there alone. I also had a growing sense that it was time for me to leave. I can't explain it.

"One morning, I came across a place where the slope of the valley wall was much more gentle than anywhere else I had been, and I just climbed out of the valley. I don't know why really. I didn't think about it.

"At first, the jungle I was passing through didn't seem any different from the jungle where I had been living in the valley. I just kept walking, not heading anywhere particularly. I had been walking all day, and the cool of evening was starting to settle in when I saw something that stopped me in my tracks. It was a small bird, lying dead beside the path. It had a broken wing and some other injuries, but whether it had been killed by some animal, had flown into something accidentally, or had dropped out of the sky due to a heart attack or some other natural disease, I did not know. But it stopped me. It occurred to me that in all the months I had spent in that valley, I had not seen any dead thing—not a bird or an animal or even an insect.

"I wanted to go back then, wanted to go back more than I had ever wanted anything in my life.

"I turned around to head back to the valley, and I saw a massive orange glow. I thought it was perhaps the setting sun reflecting off the clouds. Then, with a shock, I realized it was a massive fire, blocking my way back. A massive forest fire. I could not go back."

"What did you do?" Devon asked.

"I did not think it safe to stay there, so I went in the opposite direction, away from the fire. The glow from the fire gave me light to keep walking well into the night. Then, I lay down to rest. I woke up shivering in the cool dawn, then I got up and kept walking. I tried to go on in the same direction, but the terrain was uneven and the jungle thick, so I often had to go off to one side or another.

"After a few days, I came across a path. I followed that until it joined another, wider path, and eventually I came to a small village. The people were friendly, but I could not speak the language. By hand gestures, they directed me to continue on the path to the next village, and there I found some aid workers. They brought me back out to civilization."

"That must have been quite an experience," Devon said.

"Yes, but here's the thing," John answered. "When I got back to civilization, I was determined to find the valley again. I didn't know where it was, of course, but I thought that the forest fire might provide a clue. I went to the government and found what we would call the forestry department and asked them about recent fires. They said there had been none. I asked them to check farther, into neighboring countries even, but they said there had been none. They had just been through the rainy season. I don't know if they were lying, but there was nothing I could do. I went so far as to hire a bush plane and fly out in the direction I thought I might have come from, but it was no use. The valleys all looked alike from the air."

"Maybe if you organized an expedition from here..." Devon began.

"No, I think not."

"Because the university won't support it? That doesn't matter. You could get a grant from a private foundation. If you could describe some of those new insects you found, you could probably get a grant."

"No," John said. "I am certain I can't go back there." He paused. "I don't know why I was allowed to go there the first time—except perhaps because I was already half-dead. Or maybe it was because I was alone in the world and near the end of my career and hadn't made the discoveries I was looking for yet. Maybe it was because I already had a bit of a reputation for being an outsider and free thinker, and it was obvious I wouldn't be believed if I did try to tell someone."

"But you told the university, and you told me," Devon said.

"The university didn't believe me," John said. "And neither do you."

"Well..." Devon squirmed. "It does sound more like...like..."

"It sounds more like something out of ancient myths than a scientific exploration of the world?"

"Well, yes."

"Precisely," John concluded.

The Lord
and the Servant

With the curtains now pulled back, the early morning sun shone in through massive windows. Light and warmth poured over Adam's bed. Adam stirred, stretched, and yawned. He got out of bed and made his way to the adjoining bathroom, where newly poured water sparkled in the tub.

A few minutes later, he emerged from the bath, refreshed and clean, and wrapped himself in an enveloping, soft, white towel. Returning to the spacious bedroom, he saw his bed had been made and clean clothes laid out on the bed. A black and white figure was briefly visible exiting through the bedroom door.

The clothes on the bed were comfortable, well tailored, sensible, and serviceable. As he dressed, Adam inspected his appearance in the full-length mirror. Sometimes he wished his clothes were more...well, flamboyant, clothes that would make him appear even more handsome than he already was.

Descending to the dining room, he found his breakfast laid out for him on the table, and the same black and white figure retreating into the kitchen. There were muffins still steaming from the oven, fresh fruit, cheese, and juice. Everything was delicious and nourishing and attractively presented. Still, Adam felt an inner craving for something a little sweeter and stickier, something dripping with chocolate.

Having breakfasted, Adam decided to take a walk through the estate grounds. The grounds were extensive, with neatly trimmed hedges, creatively arranged and thoroughly weeded flower beds, and shady paths through green woodlands. Adam's walk was pleasant and invigorating.

Returning from his walk, Adam approached the west wall of the palace. Facing him was a vast wall of intricate stonework and beautiful stained glass windows.

"There really should be a door in this wall," Adam reflected.

Reflecting further, he reached a decision. Though gifted in many ways, Jeeves was an unsatisfactory servant, too prone to want things his own way.

Adam turned along the wall toward the door inset at the corner of the building. It was an unsatisfactory place for a door, Adam had often thought.

Entering the first floor study, Adam pulled the servant's bell cord. Immediately, the familiar black and white figure of Jeeves appeared.

"Jeeves," Adam said, "I have decided to dismiss you."

"Dismiss me?"

"Yes. I have concluded that you are not a good servant."

"On the contrary, I am a very good servant."

"No, you are not a good servant. You do not do what I tell you. I tell you to buy me elegant clothes, and you buy me sensible, serviceable clothes. I order sweet, sticky buns for breakfast, and you buy me muffins and fruit. I tell you to have a door opened in the west wall, and you do not have it done."

"Ah, I see. You believe that this is your palace and your estate and I am your servant. You are mistaken. You are an honored guest here, and I have been commanded to care for you and give you what you need. However, this is not your palace nor your estate. They belong to my Lord, and I am his servant, not yours. I obey his orders, not yours."

Report from Banduria

"I want to thank you for inviting my wife and me into your home."

"No problem. We are glad to do it," Jason replied. "As you know, our faith requires us to show hospitality to those who are traveling, especially to those who are messengers of the gospel."

"Hebrews 13:2," Andrew replied. "Do not neglect to show hospitality to strangers, for by this some have entertained angels without knowing it." He smiled. "Speaking of that, what did you think of our presentation at church this morning?"

"Oh, it was good," Jason answered. "I thought you gave a good summary of your work in the country of Banduria." He paused. "In fact, if you don't mind, I would like to ask you a question about that."

"Certainly."

"You probably don't remember me, but I was there when you made your first presentation in our church about twenty years ago. I was only in high school, but it made quite an impression on me. I still remember it."

"I'm impressed," Andrew answered. "I must have seemed a little young and naïve back then."

"No, no. On the contrary, I thought you made a very clear presentation of how God had called you and Marjorie to go and evangelize the country of Banduria. You talked about the ethnic makeup of the country, its social and economic problems, and how the country was only five percent Christian."

"You have a good memory," Andrew said. "You probably remember that better than I do."

"I committed myself to pray for you," Jason said. "And I have continued to pray for you and your work for the past twenty years."

"I am very grateful for that," Andrew said. "You are indeed a prayer warrior."

"Well, here's the thing," Jason said leaning forward. "I listened to your presentation this morning. You described the people of the country in a little more detail than you did the first time. You described the social and economic problems on a little deeper level. And you talked about how the country is only five percent Christian."

"Yes," Andrew encouraged.

"Well," Jason said. "You said you were going to go as a missionary to the country of Banduria and you were going to evangelize that country. You've been there twenty years, I've been praying for you all that time, and the country is still only five percent Christian. Nothing has changed."

Andrew pondered that a moment. "Well, I wouldn't say that nothing has changed. You do remember me talking about our work in the town of Hangor Baxa. There were no Christian churches in that area when we went there, and now there are seven."

"Yes, I understand that," Jason said. "But you only started four of those. Three were started by members of the first four churches."

"I also talked about the school, the orphanage, the medical center, and the Bible college we started," Andrew said, "as well as the economic program to provide employment for women."

"Oh, yes, I heard all of that," Jason answered. "It is very impressive as far as it goes. You seem to have made a significant impact on the town of Hangor Baxa and the area around it."

"So, what is the problem?"

"Well," Jason said. "There are now, what, a few hundred more Christians in Banduria than there were when you went out the first time, out of a population of three and a half million."

"About that," Andrew conceded.

"It's just that I had expected more than that. The first time you were here, you talked about the whole population of Banduria, and you said you were going to evangelize that country."

"Yes," Andrew said.

"But you didn't do that. You only evangelized part of Hangor Baxa, which is itself only a small and not very important town in that country. You can't be said to have had any impact at all on the country as a whole."

Andrew thought about that for a bit. "I see your point. I suppose I should have said that I was going as a missionary to evangelize in the town of Hangor Baxa rather than as a missionary to the country of Banduria. But when we first went there, we had to spend some time learning the local language and doing some investigative work to see where the best place was to make a start. We didn't know much about Hangor Baxa or any other town specifically when we first went there."

"Please don't think that I am criticizing you," Jason said. "When I think about it, I am impressed with what you have accomplished. I just expected more somehow."

Andrew thought for a moment. "Andrew, do you mind if I ask you a question?"

"Sure."

"When I left here for Banduria, it was said that the population of our country was about seventy percent Christian, although probably a little less than half of that percentage were practicing Christians, real believers."

"Yes, I think that is right," Jason said.

"Well, when I came back this time, I looked at some survey numbers, and only about sixty percent of the population consider themselves Christian, and only about twenty percent regularly attend a Christian church."

"I suppose that is true," Jason said.

"Well," Andrew answered. "All of that time I have been evangelizing in Banduria, you have been here in this country. Why haven't you done a better job of evangelizing this country?"

"That's a hard question," Jason said. "It is a big country, larger than Banduria. I do talk to my neighbors and some of the people I work with about Jesus. I witness to my family members. I have written letters to the editor of several newspapers talking about Christianity. I donate to my church and to Christian organizations. But I am only one person. I have limited time and resources. I am only in contact with a limited number of people. There is only so much one person can do."

"I feel the same way," Andrew said. "When I see the great need in a country like Banduria, I want to help as much as I can. But there is only so much one person can do." He paused. "But I think that is what the kingdom of God is like. Perhaps we should stop talking about evangelizing countries or people groups. The kingdom of God is not built one country at a time or one government at a time. It is built one person at a time. I think that is the way Jesus intended it."

Death

Isaac looked through the window in the door before entering the room. Some late afternoon sun was leaking in through pinholes in the curtains, barely illuminating walls of a pale, indeterminate color and a gray, tiled floor. There were no paintings or other wall decorations, and in the corner only a single, uncomfortable-looking chair. A bed draped in stark, white sheets dominated the room.

Isaac breathed deeply, pushed the door open, and walked in. The room, like the hall outside, smelled of medicine and disinfectant. Isaac took another deep breath and slowly approached the prone figure in the high, white bed. For a few moments, he looked down at the man, who appeared to be asleep. His eyes were closed, and his breathing was soft and shallow.

"Mr. Bradford," Isaac said quietly.

At first, he thought the man had not heard. Then, the eyes slowly opened.

"Mr. Bradford," Isaac repeated, "I am Pastor Abrahams. Would you like to talk for a few minutes?"

The man in the bed remained silent for a few moments and then replied in a voice that was weak but clearer than Isaac had expected.

"Pastor Abrahams. Yes." And then, after another pause, "Why don't you pull up the chair and sit down? If you could crank up the bed for me, we could still see each other while we talk."

Nothing further was said as Isaac pulled the large, low, uncomfortable chair into position and cranked up the head of the bed. The figure in the bed did not move but watched Isaac intently with his eyes.

When he had sat down in the chair, Isaac picked up the conversation again. "As I was saying, I am Pastor Abrahams. You can call me Isaac if you like."

"I think I would rather call you Pastor," replied the figure in the bed unexpectedly.

Isaac was a bit startled by the suddenness of the response but said—he hoped he had retained his relaxed tone of voice—"As you like." Then, he added, by way of getting the conversation more on track, "Your sister Sarah asked me to come and see you. She is a member of my congregation."

"Yes, I had asked if I could speak to someone."

"I see," Isaac said. "Of course, I have learned from your sister that you have been ill for some time."

"Cancer," the figure in the bed replied. It was strange how emotionless the word was when he said it. Normally, from healthy people, the word dripped with fear, horror, and anxiety.

"Did you wish me to pray for you, that you will be healed?"

The figure in the bed did not reply directly. "Pastor," he said, "the first doctor told me I had cancer over three years ago. Since then, I have had two major operations and months of treatment. All that time, my relatives have been praying for healing. Even I prayed for healing. Once even a chaplain came in."

Isaac thought of the several times Sarah had asked for prayer for her brother at prayer meetings in the church, prayer that he would be healed both physically and spiritually.

"They won't do any more operations, Pastor. There is no point in praying for healing either. It's too late for that now. I'm dying."

The plain words had now been spoken. Isaac had known people to face unwelcome truths before, but rarely had he heard the truth expressed so clearly, so starkly.

"In that case," Isaac said after a few moments of silence, "what is it you wanted to talk about?"

"I want to prepare for death," the figure in the bed replied.

"Ah, then may I ask you how you have lived? What is your faith?"

"I have not been a church member. When my sisters decided to become Christians, I did not."

Isaac knew all this from Sarah's prayer requests. "What of your life then? How have you lived?"

"I worked most of my life—until this. I had a steady job as a meatcutter. It was honest work. I have never broken the law or done anything really bad, but..." He paused.

"But you're not sure you're ready to die and meet God, is that it?" Isaac asked.

"Yes."

"Let me clarify your problem a little by asking you another question. What has been the purpose of your life?"

"Purpose?" the figure inquired. "I don't have any calling or great life's work if that's what you mean. I wasn't any Albert Schweitzer or Mother Teresa."

"No. Not many of us are." Isaac smiled. "What I meant was: What motivated you? What did you want out of life? What made you get out of bed in the morning?"

The eyes focused on the far wall as if the figure was seeing something that was not there, like a rerun of an old movie. "I enjoyed myself. I had a lot of good things in my life. Friends, money. I enjoyed cars and sports," he said. "I'm grateful for those, though," he added hopefully.

"I see," said Isaac. "So, basically, you lived for yourself?"

"Yes, I guess so, though it seems rather harsh if you put it that way. I did help some people. I gave to charity sometimes, did favors for friends, loved my family."

"As long as those things did not interfere too much with your personal enjoyment of life?"

"I, ah...." Bradford seemed confused by the question.

"What I mean," Isaac said, "is that you did not, for instance, sell your car so that you could give the money to the poor."

"Well, no."

"And if your sister Sarah was dying of cancer, you would not spend every evening and weekend sitting with her."

"Well, no. That's a lot to ask," he said after a pause.

"Yes, but that's love. It's what Jesus did for us. He gave up heaven and came to earth, where He spent His life teaching and healing. And then He died for us."

"He died for us?" Bradford interrupted.

"Yes, He died for us. Oh, it's not that we won't all die," Isaac continued as if he had just understood the meaning of the question. "We will all die, but if we commit ourselves to Jesus, then death will not be permanent. We will live again with Jesus in heaven."

"Yes," Bradford replied. "That's what I want. I want to live again in heaven. How do I commit myself to Jesus?"

"Well, you must first accept His offer of forgiveness for all of the things you have done wrong or not done that you should have done. You must accept that He died in your place, as punishment for the things you have done wrong, and that you can live again in heaven because Jesus rose again from the dead. You can be resurrected because He was resurrected and you want to follow Him."

"Yes," Bradford replied. "I want to follow Jesus and be resurrected."

"There is something else," Isaac said. "Jesus is both our Savior and our Lord. You must also say, 'Jesus, from now on, You are my Lord, my Boss'—or 'my Commanding Officer.' More than that even. You must say, 'Jesus, I will do anything You want. I will serve You. I will even give up my life. I will die if that's what You want.' Mr. Bradford, are you willing to do that?"

Bradford was silent a moment before replying. "Yes," he said finally. "I will do that. I have accepted that I am going to die. I am ready to commit myself to Jesus."

Bradford looked expectantly at Isaac as if waiting for the next step, the completion of a process or a negotiation they seemed to have been involved in.

But Isaac was silent for what seemed like several minutes as if listening or thinking. At last, he looked up into Bradford's eyes, which had not wavered. "There is one catch," he said finally.

Bradford's eyes reflected a cold flush of concern, but he said nothing.

Isaac continued, "When you first became sick, your sister asked our church to pray for your healing. When we pray, we ask God to do things, but we do not control the answer. That is up to Him. Jesus did not choose to heal you earlier when our church prayed for you, back when it seemed possible. But now that it is impossible...well, Jesus has the habit of performing great miracles for those who commit themselves to Him. He even raised several people from the dead to return to living on this earth for a while longer. Of course, I can't guarantee anything, but I have to warn you. If you decide to commit yourself to Jesus, there is the possibility that Jesus will heal you of your cancer. You might have another thirty or forty years to live on this earth, and if you were committed to Jesus, you couldn't go on living the kind of self-centered life you have been living up to now. You would have to open yourself up to living the same kind of self-sacrificing, loving life that Jesus lived for us. You are ready to die with Jesus, but are you willing to live for Him?"

A Family Story

Robert Aaron Douglas was born in 1925. As a result, he grew up dirt poor, on a farm, in the middle of the Great Depression. He was the last of six children, three boys and three girls. As the few surviving photos reveal, the tone of that era was black and white, or brown and gray. Like most folks in those days, the family went to the local church when the weather was good and they had gas for the truck. The church was the center of the community, but other than that, it didn't mean a great deal. They just took church for granted. It was hard to believe in anything back then.

Robert, now called Bob, joined the army in 1943. His older brother Tom was killed on D-Day, but Bob was one of the luckier ones. He returned home and married a girl from the next farm, Sandra Foster, in 1948. Bob had grown up tinkering with the farm tractor, the army had trained him as a mechanic, and he soon had a job at a local garage. Bob and Sandy moved into a bungalow in town. They had three children, Barbara in 1949, Douglas in late 1950, and Jenny in 1953. The family went to church regularly. It was a hopeful time. Bob was an usher and later served on the church board for eight years. Sandy taught Sunday school and went to ladies' aid meetings in the afternoons when the children were in school.

Barb was the one most infected with hope. When she grew up, she went overseas to work on a development project in an undeveloped country, digging wells and providing basic health care. She found it very fulfilling and stayed. She never married. She died in 2003 after contracting a fever.

Jenny was the rebel. In the 1960s, she discovered bell bottoms and tie-dyed T-shirts. She went to Woodstock in 1969 and discovered a whole new world. She never returned home. She went west and joined a commune for a time. The family lost track of her for a while. They would still hear from her now and then. She died of a drug overdose in 1987. It took the authorities two months to find and notify her family.

Bob died of a heart attack in 1993. Sandy lingered longer, dying from cancer in 2005. She had been a faithful member of the church all her life and was one of the last members of the ladies' aid to pass.

Bob and Sandy's middle child, Douglas, was the first one in his family to go to university, and he chose a university in the nearest city about fifty miles away. On his third Saturday night on campus, he got drunk, and he slept in the next morning. He never went to church again. In the middle of his third year, he met Sofia Bulgers. They moved in together shortly afterwards. Her father was a Pentecostal minister. They got married after graduation in 1971 to satisfy their parents. Sofia obtained an administrative position in the counseling department, while Doug went on to graduate school. In time, he became a professor of comparative religion at a university farther from home. His most prominent book was *HOPE: How the Octopus Principle Enervates All Religions.* An adoring critic described it as "a provocative book whose thesis defies definition." Sofia became a devotee of Buddhism. They eventually drifted apart, and their divorce, finalized in 1994, two years short of their silver anniversary, was acrimonious. A short time later, Sofia's place in Doug's bed was taken by Daniella Storm, a twenty-three-year-old graduate student. The relationship lasted three years, six months and five days, ending when Daniella finished her degree. Sofia concluded that all men were pigs and developed a long-term lesbian relationship with her yoga instructor. Doug's job performance became increasingly erratic, and he was pushed into early retirement in 2010.

Along the way, before their marriage collapsed, Doug and Sofia produced two children. Trevor was born in the fall of 1971, and Angela in 1976. Trevor moved out right after high school when a family friend got him a job as an electrician's apprentice back in the smaller city where he had been born and where his father had first gone to university as a student. Two years later, a girl named Rosa moved in with him. They were not married but produced three children.

As her parents' marriage disintegrated, Angela became confused and angry. She did not come home some nights and eventually dropped out of school, living on the streets. Doug and Sofia barely noticed. Angela became addicted to drugs, and Sofia blamed Doug since "addiction ran in his family." In 1996, Angela was arrested for armed robbery and sentenced to four years in prison. Two years later, she was convicted of assault, which added another year to her sentence. Back on the street, she was hospitalized in 2004 after a severe beating. Already suffering from cancer, Sandy visited her granddaughter in the hospital and convinced her to go to House of Hope, a Christian facility for street women back in the university city where Doug had earned his first degree. Six months later, Angela had a profound experience with Jesus Christ. Through a House of Hope program, she was able to complete high school and got a job in a bakery. The minister at the small church she had begun attending convinced her to participate in FM101 ("Tune in to Jesus and 'Follow Me'"), an eight-month discipleship program. Here, she was able to deal with her pain and scars and find healing.

Angela's brother Trevor, whom she had not seen for several years, attended her "graduation celebration" from FM101. The fact was that his relationship with Rosa was falling apart, and he was drowning. Angela convinced him to enroll in the next session of FM101. It changed his life. He became a Christian believer, was baptized, and joined a church. Rosa wanted nothing to do with this "religious thing." However, the change in Trevor's behavior gradually brought her around. Two years later, Rosa and their oldest daughter, Maria, were baptized and joined the church where Angela and Trevor were members. Two years after that, in 2010, Maria went off to Bible school.

In 2015, Angela brought her father, Doug, now unable to care for himself, to live with her. He died of heart failure in 2017. There was enough money left in his estate for Angela to use as a down payment for a small house. By this time, Angela had upgraded her training in night school and was manager of the small bakery, so she was able to cover the mortgage payments. She began opening her home to women who had graduated from House of Hope and were now transitioning back into society.

Sofia had moved, and the family was never able to track her down.

Rosa died of cancer in 2023, and in 2025 Trevor married Tanya, a widow lady in the church.

Trevor and Rosa's oldest daughter, Maria, met a young man named Rick Brown in Bible college. They are now married with three children. Rick is pastor of a church in a town a couple of hundred miles away.

Trevor and Rosa's second child, Aaron, went to university and became an accountant. He and his wife Nora have two children. Aaron leads a boys' club at the church.

Trevor and Rosa's third child, Andrea, is now in her late twenties and has not yet found herself.

It is the times we live in and the choices we make that determine our lives.

I suppose, if I were a serious writer, I could turn this family history into a novel, or maybe a series of novels, but that would involve describing a lot of unnecessary details—the cars they drove, the color of the dresses and shirts they wore, and the evolution of their kitchen appliances. I have told you the important things.

Health Fails, Simpkins Passes

Well-known theologian Dr. Thomas Simpkins passed away November 31 at his home in Layaway, Georgia.

He was born Simpkins Tompkins but, for reasons never made clear, later changed his name to Thomas Simpkins.

He began his studies at Fundamentalist Baptist Bible College in Narroway, Texas, earning a Bachelor of Evangelical and Systematic Theology degree. He went on to earn a Master of Interdenominational Divinity degree from Via Media School of Theology, completing his academic studies by earning a Doctorate in Inter-Faith Formation from the Darwinian Institute of Religious Thought.

For a while, he had held a half-time position at Total Commitment Ministries, but, after completing his studies, he was appointed assistant professor in the prestigious Department of Eastern Philosophy and Western Enlightenment at Northwestern University of the Global South. He remained there for the rest of his career, eventually rising to the position of Assistant Provost of Education. After being given the status of professor emeritus nine years ago, he was rarely seen at the university.

Simpkins is best known for the development of the theory of Nonessential Theology. His argument was that since "the devil is in the details," what matters in theology is not the study of great themes such as justification and sanctification but the more peripheral issues of how these concepts might or might not be applied.

Later critics downplayed the originality and significance of Nonessential Theology, arguing that it was not that different from what other theologians were doing.

Simpkins' best known books were *Nonessential Theology*, *Nonessential Theology Revisited*, *Nonessential Theology Reconsidered*, *The Gospel According to Buddha*, and *The Gospel According to Jerry Springer*.

Students remember Simpkins best for the repetitive tediousness of his lectures, but Simpkins averred that this style was deliberate, citing the old adage, "Anything worth saying is worth repeating, more than once or twice, if necessary, and it is better to say a good thing twice than not to say it at all."

Simpkins is survived by his ex-wives Faith, Hope, and Joy; his children Ulysses, Demeter, Epicurus, and Persephone; and 57 grandchildren.

The life of Dr. Simpkins was remembered in a public memorial at the university and in a private family service on Crableg Beach near his seafront home. His ashes were scattered by the premature arrival of hurricane season.

My Friend E and the Great Inter-Faith Prayer Meeting

My friend E has just returned from the National Inter-Faith Prayer Meeting for Drought Relief. He said it was a wonderful experience. I give E a lot of credit. The meeting was held at the Carmel High Place, and it must have taken a lot of grace on his part to go to such an event at a retreat center owned by another religious tradition.

Most of the major religions in our country were represented there, which says something about how serious the current drought really is. We haven't had rain for some years, there are few crops except for what we can grow by irrigation, and now the wells and streams are going dry. The cattle, sheep, and other livestock are dying. People are dying of starvation, malnourishment, and disease. We wonder why the people in other countries don't send us aid. After all, we share some of the same religions they have in their countries.

At the prayer meeting, it had been agreed ahead of time that each faith group would lead in prayers and worship for one session, using their own forms and traditions.

As representatives of the oldest national religion, the native peoples had the privilege of leading the first session. The Canaanite priestesses (setting a wonderful example of the equality of men and women in religious leadership) first erected a "grove" of poles to the fertility goddess Asherah. Then women presented cakes to Asherah, symbols of the food that we hope will be produced again when the rains return. Finally, men representing the Lord Baal went into the center of the grove and had ritual sex with temple prostitutes. This symbolic act represented the sky god Baal coming down darkly in clouds and injecting semen (rain) into the earth goddess Asherah to make her fertile and fruitful.

This, of course, set the stage for the next session, led by the 400 prophets of Baal. They put on quite a spectacle. They really know how to involve the whole person, body and soul, in worship, and there is much we can learn from them. They danced and shouted and cut themselves till the blood flowed down onto the ground, again symbolic of Baal sending rain to make the ground fertile again. The dancing and shouting are considered necessary to gain Baal's attention because he is busy with other parts of the earth and, since he can't be everywhere at once, he may forget about us if we don't do something to remind him that we are here and we need his help. The climax of their presentation was the sacrificing of a bull on a large altar of stones. The bull represents the powerful god Baal, and its exceptional flow of semen represents the powerful rain that a great god like Baal can pour out to fertilize the earth.

In a very solemn session led by the priests of Molech, three children were sacrificed and burned on an altar. This represented the seriousness of our situation. Unless God sends rain, we and all of our children are going to die.

The event continued in that way, with processions and rituals and prayers offered by various traditions, including believers in Chemosh, Bel, and Marduk. One session included male shrine prostitutes, which shows how far we have come, how tolerant we now are. All segments of our society were represented at the event.

Finally, it was E's turn. (It's strange really. Everyone just calls him E. In fact, we have been calling him that for so long that I can't remember what his full name is. I wonder if he remembers.) Anyway, E performed the traditional ritual of the sacrifice of a bull in honor of the Israelite tribal god Yahweh. After some of the other, more elaborate presentations, this must have seemed a bit of an anticlimax. Still, I don't know what else he could have done. He is the only prophet of Yahweh remaining and didn't have a lot of resources available.

The king graciously thanked all of the religious representatives for coming and praised them for agreeing to join together in this way. Although he did not hide his own preference for Baal worship, everyone was treated with the greatest respect. He is truly a wise, enlightened, and competent king.

Surely, God must have been pleased with this National Inter-Faith Prayer Meeting. (I hear more inter-faith services are being planned for the future.) He must be very happy when his children unite in peace. It is probably too early to say for sure, of course. Unfortunately, God does not seem to have answered yet. The drought continues, and there is no sign of rain.

The General

"You wished to see me, Commander?"

"Yes, General. I want to know how the assault on the village of Salem is progressing."

The General hesitated. "Well, Commander, we are making some progress, but we have also suffered some casualties. There were originally seventy defenders of the village."

"Yes, yes, I know the figures. Your task was to conquer the village and kill those seventy defenders. I gave you ten thousand soldiers to accomplish that task. Now, tell me what progress you have made."

"Yes, Commander. I assembled my men and surrounded the village. Then I spoke to the defenders and offered them the opportunity to surrender and to come over to our side and serve you, Commander. I promised them that they would not be harmed and would prosper under your sovereignty. That was a lie. I would have killed them later, of course. However, they are a very disciplined group and not one of them would agree to leave the side of that rebel farmer who leads them. Not one of them would agree to come over to our side. So, after several futile attempts to persuade them, I ordered my soldiers to attack them."

"Good, good. And did your men kill them?"

"As I said, Commander, we have made some progress."

"Progress?"

"Yes. We have killed twenty-five of them."

"Twenty-five only? You have vastly superior members and weapons. Why did you not succeed in killing them all? Did they mount a strong resistance?"

"Not exactly, Commander. In fact, the seventy defenders did not mount a defense at all, in one sense. They did not use any weapons, although some did try to flee and avoid the blows of my soldiers."

"Some?"

"Yes. Some others just stood there and accepted the blows of my soldiers."

"Then why did your soldiers not succeed in killing them all?"

"Well, my soldiers are hardened fighters and brave men, but they had never before encountered an enemy who did not fight back, and some of them were reluctant to kill men who just stood there. And then there was the argument factor."

"The argument factor?"

"Yes. The enemy leader, their general, had trained them well. He had given them words. They began to speak to our soldiers. They asked them what they were doing and why they were killing, why they were on our side, why…."

"Words, words—you can't stop swords with words. So, why didn't your soldiers succeed in killing the villagers?"

"Well, they convinced some of our soldiers that it would not be a good idea to kill them."

"Convinced? Not a good idea!? These are soldiers. They are supposed to obey orders. Why didn't you make them obey? Or why didn't you just send other soldiers to do the killing?"

"Yes, Commander. I did that, but I had to use my men strategically, in order to keep the number of casualties down."

"Casualties?" How could there be casualties? I thought you said the villagers did not fight back?"

"Yes, Commander. They did not fight back, except with their words and their deeds."

"Deeds? So they did fight back?"

"No, Commander. They did not fight. You see, one of my men who was chasing one of the villagers, stumbled and fell.

A clumsy fellow, he fell on his own sword and was wounded."

"So, the villager turned around and killed him?"

"No, Commander. The villager turned back and began to dress our soldier's wounds—he was bleeding quite profusely and probably would have died. The villager saved his life. There were several such incidents. Two more of our soldiers fell into the river and might have drowned, their armor pulling them down, if the villagers had not pulled them out to safety."

"But if the villagers saved their lives, then there were no casualties. What are you talking about, General?"

"I am afraid, sir, that between their words and their deeds, the villagers convinced some of our soldiers to switch to their side."

"But why? Didn't our soldiers understand that if they switched sides, they, too, would be killed? You should have executed them as traitors."

"Yes, sir. They understood that they were signing their own death warrants, but they chose to switch anyway. One said that he would rather die with the villagers than kill with our soldiers."

"I see the problem. These soldiers who switched to the side of the villagers, they were trained soldiers, and so they fought back, defending the villagers and killing our soldiers."

"No, Commander. As soon as these soldiers switched their loyalty to the other side, they, too, put down their weapons."

"Then why did you not order our other soldiers to kill them?"

"I did, Commander, but the disloyal soldiers picked up the words of the villagers and began to persuade more of our soldiers not to kill."

"But they had just switched sides. Surely, these disloyal soldiers had not learned many of the rebel general's words. They would not have been persuasive. Perhaps you could even have tried to persuade them to come back to our side—especially if you threatened them with death."

"I did, Commander, but to a man they all refused to come back. But you are wrong, Commander, in thinking that they had not yet learned enough of the rebel general's words to be effective in argument. In fact, some of them were even more persuasive than the original villagers had been. They knew our soldiers, were friends with them…In fact, several times I was forced to order a strategic withdrawal in order to prevent whole battalions of our soldiers being lost to the other side."

"This is very disturbing. But you have not abandoned the attack? You are still attempting to kill the villagers?"

"Yes, Commander, but the outcome is far from certain."

"What is the situation, then? You said you had already killed—what was it?—twenty-five of the villagers?"

"Yes, Commander. We have killed over a third of the villagers. Yet, we also have suffered heavy casualties. The villagers have persuaded one hundred and forty-three of our soldiers to switch to their side."

"One hundred and forty-three! But that means…."

"Yes, Commander. There are now more than twice as many villagers as there were when we began the attack."

"This is serious. Perhaps it was a mistake to attack the villagers. You should probably have seized the rebel general and killed him first."

"Yes, Commander, I have ordered my soldiers to do that now, but…."

"But what?"

"I don't know how, but I have a growing fear that if we do kill the rebel general, that, too, may backfire."

"Preposterous!"

The Enemy

It was in January that he had come floating down to them out of a black sky, like the demon he undoubtedly was. His arrival followed by a few minutes the din of explosions in the city forty miles away. Hours later, long after they had finished the deed, a red glow remained in the sky in the direction in which the city had been, a city that had housed their cousins, their fellow patriots, and, in some cases, their own grown-up children.

It was Gustav who had seen him first, hanging from his parachute in a tree on the edge of the woods behind the house. Gustav had gone out to check on the last livestock remaining in the barn. So many had gone to feed the brave soldiers, those patriots who defended them and their farms, their wives, and their children from the enemy. They had heard about the enemy over the wireless, how they slaughtered women and children, assaulted innocent young girls, and stole food from the aged. They understood that the enemy must be madmen to practice such cruelty, men possessed by demons, servants of the devil himself. The local militia commander himself had confirmed the stories they had heard over the open air. He emphasized how evil the enemy must be every time he came and commandeered their cattle to feed the heroic soldiers of the fatherland or took away their sons to be soldiers themselves or came to inform them, with a sad countenance, that their sons would not be coming back. They understood how evil the enemy must be to do such awful things. The commander himself had told them. That is why, later, they did not understand.

With fear in his heart, Gustav had run back to the house. One of the enemy was hanging in the tree! After pausing briefly to cry out a warning, he had thought of his neighbors and had run through the village, banging on doors and crying out like a madman, "The enemy is in the tree!"

With axes and scythes in their hands, they had stumbled out of their rude dwellings, agitated with fear. Where? Where are the enemy? Shall we run? How many are there? What will happen to our wives and children?

Quickly but unevenly, Gustav had led them toward the trees behind his house. The enemy had climbed down out of the tree and was standing somewhat unsteadily, rubbing his shoulder. What would he do to them? Would he devour them with fire as he had the city? Would he rip them apart with metal bullets and exploding shells as he had their patriotic sons who had gone away and never returned? Slowly, he had raised his hands above his head. With a cry of fear, they had surged forward, striking blindly with axes and scythes, driven in their desperation to save their lives by the extremity of their fury.

It was only when the enemy was a shapeless mass on the ground, unrecognizable as anything human, that they had ceased to strike at him. And then, without talking, they had done what their ancestors had done since time immemorial to the most fearful incursions of evil among them. They had burned the enemy in a great bonfire of branches and logs, blotting him out forever from the face of the earth. They had felt satisfied, and that is why they could not understand.

It was the fire that brought the commander to them in his old touring car, with two or three of his militiamen.

"What have you done?" he cried.

"We have killed the enemy," they replied proudly.

"You should have brought him to me!"

"But he would have killed us!" they cried in fear.

"No. He would not have killed you. He was only one man."

"If he is as evil as you say, he would have killed us," they insisted.

"But you should not have killed him. He should have been captured. We should have made him a prisoner of war. My superiors will not like this at all."

"If he is as evil as you say, he should have been killed," they repeated stubbornly.

The discussion had gone on for hours until the red glow from the burned-out city had almost faded from the sky. At last, with an angry speech denouncing them as fools and madmen and traitors to the fatherland, he had stumped back to his car and driven away.

The villagers stood still and silent beside the glowing ashes. Finally, Gustav spoke. "If it is wrong to kill the enemy, the enemy must not be as evil as they say," he said. Silently, they separated and returned to their homes.

Surely the People

"The train is ready for boarding," the official said.

Peter and Andrew rose heavily to their feet and began moving toward the platform. But the official stood in front of them, staring into their faces, as if there were more to be done or said.

"You will not come back," he said.

"No," they answered.

It had not been a question.

"You believe you are going to your promised land?" the official continued.

"Yes, our God loves us and will bless us."

"You?" he asked. "Why you?"

"Because we are his people," Peter replied. "We are Peter and Andrew, named after his chief followers. We have been his people since birth." He paused. "We are his people," he repeated.

The official was silent a moment.

"And us?" he said.

"You are not one of us. You are not his people. The new land does not belong to you."

"You would not invite me to join you, would you?"

"The new land..." Andrew said. "You would not want to come."

"In the new land," Peter added curtly, "we will have no need of officials."

They knew this official, Peter and Andrew. He had lived near their village, but he was not one of them. They did not know his name. They did not wish to know.

"You know nothing of the new land," Peter continued. "You are an ignorant man."

The official looked into their eyes one more time. "I'm glad you are going," he said. Then, he slowly, deliberately stepped aside so they could pass.

They walked out onto the platform and followed the other passengers into the train. They stowed their baggage under their seats and settled down onto the hard benches. Turning, they saw the face of the official at the window. Without taking his eyes from the official, Andrew lowered the window.

The official smiled a half smile and looked again into their eyes. "Surely you are the people," he said, "and wisdom will depart with you."

He turned abruptly and disappeared into the station. After a moment, the train jerked and slowly moved out of the station, gathering momentum as it went.

Inside, the train, Andrew stared straight ahead of him. "What do you suppose he meant by that?" he said.

"He recognized who we are," Peter replied. "Even the officials must recognize the true people in the end."

"Yes, I suppose," Andrew admitted. After a moment, he added, "But it seemed like he meant something by it, a veiled suggestion he didn't think we would understand."

Peter merely grunted.

"It was like a quotation," Andrew asserted, "a quotation from a book he had studied often and knew well. He said it like it was a passage from his favorite book and he knew we wouldn't understand."

"Probably it was from one of his communist books," Peter responded firmly, sounding a little annoyed.

"Yes, but which book?" Andrew asked.

"I don't know. Perhaps we'll find it one day. Yes, someday I'll have to look for it." Peter shut his eyes and leaned back, bringing the conversation to a close.

Adam's Enterprise

Adam's enterprise was not doing well. He was failing in almost every aspect of his business. He knew he needed help and sought out many advisors, who promised help for just such a situation. These sharks and dragons offered a variety of solutions. He tried many of them. But eventually he concluded that they provided no hope. Rather than help him, their schemes would confine him more closely and impoverish him further while they became richer.

In desperation, Adam sought out the oldest and wisest advisor of all. The old man listened carefully as Adam poured out a detailed account of all of his problems and failings, his concerns and his worries.

When Adam was finished, the old man was silent for a while. Adam looked at him anxiously, holding his breath, hardly daring to hope.

Finally, the old man said, "Yes, I can help you."

Adam started breathing again.

The old man said, "This is what I will do. I will pay off all of your debts. In return, I want 51 percent of your business."

Adam gulped. He knew he was deeply in debt and could not pay what he owed. But the cost of this help was higher than he wanted to pay. "Fifty-one percent is a lot," he said. "That would mean that you would be making all of the decisions."

"That's the point," the old man said. "You have been making all of the decisions up to now, and that is what has gotten you into all of the trouble you are in. I am a lot wiser than you are."

"Yes, of course," Adam said. "But I wouldn't get to make any decisions at all. I would just be an employee, a servant."

"That is not entirely true," the old man said. "Part of the arrangement is that I would train you to make wise decisions."

"But that means I would still always be doing what you want," Adam protested.

"Yes, but what I want is what is best for you and everyone else."

"You see, there's the thing," Adam said. "Me and everyone else. Sometimes what is good for everyone else would not be good for me. What is good for someone else might end up costing me something."

"Only in the short run," the old man said. "In the long run, it would be better for everyone, including you."

"Yes, but it would still cost me some discomfort and trouble in the short run."

"It all depends on whether you are looking for a quick profit or a good, long-term investment."

"You are into long-term investments, aren't you?" Adam said.

"Yes, very long-term investments," the old man agreed. "Even eternal ones."

Lame

Embarrassed, I fell into line. I knew what was expected of me. Looking ahead, I could see the long line snaking up the hill. Our destination at the top of the steep incline could not be seen from where I was.

The sun beat down mercilessly, and I began to sweat from the weight of what I was carrying. The dust kicked up by so many shuffling feet soon covered everything.

The day dragged on, and my progress was painfully slow. The heat continued to build. Slowly, we inched forward. Mindful of the solemn occasion, everyone in line refrained from speaking. There was not much to be said.

Eventually, I reached the crest of the hill, and I could see what I had been moving toward. A long line of worshipers were still in front of me, but up ahead I could see the priest, on a small platform. He was dressed in a long, white robe that was dazzling in the sunshine. A gleaming golden headdress was on his head, and the front of his tunic was adorned with more gold and sparkling jewels. In front of the priest was a massive altar, plated with pure gold.

As they approached, the worshippers in turn placed their offerings one by one on the gleaming altar.

Finally, it was my turn. As he had said to the others, the priest intoned to me, "You must bring a sacrifice that is perfect in every way, an offering that is neither blind nor lame, neither disfigured nor deformed, a sacrifice without blemish or defect."

I looked down at what was in my arms, and I felt ashamed. I saw that what I held was hopelessly flawed, blind and maimed, broken and ruined, an unworthy offering in every sense. But what could I do? It was all I had. I did not dare to look at the priest. As quietly and unobtrusively as I could, I dumped my wholly unsuitable offering onto the altar.

I kept my eyes averted, my head down. Tears began to roll down my cheeks. I knew my offering could never be acceptable. The situation was hopeless.

Gradually, by some unseen force that was beyond my control, I could feel my eyes being slowly pulled upward, until I was staring into the stern face of the priest. I could not pull my eyes away, but I cringed as I waited for him to pronounce my offering unacceptable. I waited for him to reject my offering and to reject me.

He opened his mouth to speak. Sternly, he intoned, "You have done well. You are a good and faithful servant. Your offering has been accepted."

In disbelief, I stared dumbfounded at the man. And then my gaze slowly dropped to the altar, until I was looking once again at my miserable, unacceptable offering. I blinked, uncomprehending. There on the golden altar was my offered sacrifice. It was gleaming white in the sunshine and was perfect and whole in every way. And so was I. I bowed my head again, in gratitude this time. When I looked up again, the priest was looking kindly into my face, smiling radiantly.

Vindicated

The morning sun shone brightly into the courtyard as a light breeze stirred the leaves of the olive trees. But there was no light on Eliakim's face. Hannah watched her husband carefully. What did she see there? Confusion? Concern? Fear? Anger? Disappointment? Betrayal?

Eliakim went over to a clay jar along the wall and carefully measured a tenth of an ephah of barley flour into a clay bowl. He turned toward his wife. Without looking directly at her, he took her by the elbow and led her out through the doorway of the courtyard onto the street. Side by side, they walked along the narrow streets of the town. Other residents stopped what they were doing to watch in solemn silence as they passed.

On they went, up a slight incline. When they reached the tabernacle, they went in through the doorway into the outer courtyard. There, a priest approached them. Eliakim held out the bowl toward the priest, nodded toward his wife, but did not speak.

The priest nodded solemnly. He turned and led the couple toward the altar, where a continual fire burned. He indicated that the woman was to stand before the altar, facing it. He reached behind her head and loosened her hair from its ornamental clasp. He took the bowl from her husband, who was standing a couple of paces away, and put it into the woman's hands. The priest then went over to a large container and dipped some holy water into a small clay jar. Stooping down, he gathered some dust from the tabernacle floor and dropped it into the jar.

The priest came and stood before the woman and formally spoke the ceremonial words: "If no other man has had sexual relations with you and you have not gone astray and become impure while married to your husband, may this bitter water that brings a curse not harm you. But if you have gone astray while married to your husband and you have made yourself impure by having sexual relations with a man other than your husband—" here, he raised his hand over the woman's head—"may the Lord cause you to become a curse among your people when he makes your womb miscarry and your abdomen swell. May this water that brings a curse enter your body so that your abdomen swells or your womb miscarries."

Hannah swallowed and took a deep breath. In a clear, quiet voice, she responded, "Amen. So be it."

The priest wrote out the curse on a parchment. Holding the parchment over the clay jar, he poured more holy water onto the parchment, so that the writing washed off into the clay jar. Then, taking the bowl of grain from the woman's hands, he held it up before the altar and cast a handful of grain into the fire as a burnt offering. Finally, the priest handed the clay jar to the woman and demanded that she drink all of the bitter water. With trembling hands, Hannah took the jar and drank the contents.

With the ceremony over, Eliakim led Hannah back through the town. She kept her head down the whole way, avoiding the stares of her neighbors.

At home, she sat down on a bench, unsure of what would come next. She picked up some mending to work on, but for the most part it remained on her lap, her hands hardly moving. She was waiting, waiting for her belly to swell, alert to any imagined twitch, not speaking. Without looking, she became aware of her husband staring at her. He was sitting on the far side of the room, face immobile and expressionless, also seemingly unable to find anything to do. She shifted her position, and he raised his head. Then, when she made no further movement, he turned and stared out through the window at the fields of grain waving in the wind.

Hannah wondered what he was thinking. Was he starting to have doubts? He had seemed so sure, as if he *knew*. She herself was sure. She knew it was only a matter of time before the period of waiting would be over. How long would it be? An hour? A few hours? A day? A week? A month? A year? The wording of the curse was not specific.

After a time, he got up and moved closer to her, although she knew it was too early for him to know anything for sure. He stared at her for a long moment, the same impassive stare carved into his face, his eyes blinking occasionally.

Suddenly, she felt a twitch. Her hand instinctively went down to her abdomen. She was aware of him becoming alert. Another twitch. He came over to stand before her. *What was he thinking?* Did he want her to be guilty, she wondered—or not? Had he taken her to the priest to put his fears to rest? Or was it his jealousy that had driven him— that same onerous jealousy that had soured their relationship, that she had told herself was to blame for what she had done, that had driven her to it, that had justified it (although it was doubtful that she had believed that even at the time)? Did that jealousy demand a guilty verdict in order to be satisfied? Did he want her, need her to be guilty? It did not matter, for she was guilty. Whatever he felt now, his jealousy would be satisfied. His jealousy would come to be seen as justified. He would be proved right. She felt another twitch—it was not yet a pain, nor was there any discernible swelling, but it was a twitch. And then another.

*****

Watching, Eliakim, too, wondered whether he wanted her to be guilty. Looking past her to the rolling hills in the distance, he wondered if he had been justified in his actions. What had his motive been in taking her to the priest? He had needed to know, of course. He could not go on living with uncertainty and suspicion. But what did he *want* to know? Regardless of what the truth was, what did he *want* it to be?

Had he truly desired her to be guilty? Did he really want the unknown answer to be sin? Of the known tallies of sin and righteousness in the world, did he want this unknown factor to be added to the sin side? Was he seriously desiring an increase in the evil in the world? He who had been taught to love good and hate sin, was he really eager to discover more sin? And in wondering so, he asked himself if he was not more guilty than the woman whom he had taken to the priest.

*****

Another twitch. He was still standing over her, watching, that unreadable expression on his face, as if he was suspending judgment, waiting impartially for the verdict, whether good or evil.

What did it matter, she thought, what he wanted? It was the deed she had committed that she was being tried for. The bitter water would find the evil seed in her body and cause it to swell. It was impossible for it not to do so. Had not the great Yahweh, the God who had parted the Red Sea and drowned Pharaoh and his army, commanded it? Was He not personally concerned with her, as He was with all of His people? And would He not make sure that this test, administered by His priest in accordance with His law, would produce a true result? The Red Sea, the water. Yes. The water, which had parted for the salvation of God's people, had drowned wicked Pharaoh, who had opposed Him and His law—just as she had done. The water was judgment—for Pharaoh and for her. In that moment, she realized that she was guilty, not just in the eyes of her husband, but also before the all-seeing God. Her deed of pleasure (but mostly the pleasure of spiting her jealous husband) was open before the Almighty Yahweh, the Lord. She recognized that her deed was really an act of spite and rebellion, not just against her husband but also against the Holy and Omniscient One. He who had given her this good land, her husband, life itself, the sun streaming in through

85

the windows—it was He whom she had betrayed in her ingratitude. Before Him, she was guilty, and He would impose His just retribution.

She felt another twinge and, she thought, a twinge of pain. The pain of her guilt twisted her mouth and lowered her eyebrows.

*****

"Can I get you anything?" Almost without thinking, he had bent forward. For him, the question of guilt had passed. Concern for abstract justice had been swallowed up by concern for his wife in pain. His fellow human being was suffering here before him, one with whom he had passed many days. Married love was a small part of his concern, for what love had there been in their marriage, in their engagement even? Guilt over his part in bringing her to this position now played a larger role. It was something that, in the vast working of the universe, in the dispositions of the Almighty just God, had happened, and his only duty now was to show compassion in the circumstances.

*****

"Can I get you anything?" he repeated.
She shook her head no, wondering, as the pain passed.
The sun had passed its zenith now. Little light came in through the windows or doorway. There was too little light even to distinguish between black and white. Already, the sun was starting to decline toward the west.
The afternoon wore on, and there was no more pain, just the odd twitch, leaving her wondering.
Suddenly, he arose, took down some bread cakes from a shelf over the hearth, and brought some to her. Then, he poured some wine from a wineskin into two cups, handing one to her. She accepted this unaccustomed role for her husband because of the unusual circumstances of the day.

They ate silently and slowly, mechanically, not thinking of the food but of other things.

When they were finished, her husband put away the food and cleaned the dishes. The sun was declining now. They sat for a long time, staring out through the windows, as its slanting rays swept over the ripening fields of grain.

When the sun had turned red and its upper rim was just dropping beneath the hills, he got up, took her by the hand, and led her into the inner room. She had not thought that she would be able to sleep, but the worry of the long day had made them both weary, and soon they were sound asleep.

*****

In the morning, Hannah awoke to the sun shining in and the birds singing outside. It was a new day, and she felt for some reason that it was a special day. Then, she remembered her belly. Her eyes and her hand went down to her belly, where she expected to see swelling—but there was none. She was sure. There was no pain. There were no twitches. There was nothing. It was as if, in that morning, she was starting her life all over again. She looked up to find her husband staring at her belly and smiling warmly.

What had happened? The test had failed. There was no other explanation. The test had failed. Either Yahweh hadn't fulfilled His promise to determine the outcome or He couldn't fulfill His promise. Was the test as much a test of Yahweh as it was of her? Slowly, an idea was dawning on her. She had been taught that Yahweh was directly involved in the operations of the world, vindicating the righteous and punishing the wicked. But was He really involved? Further, did He in fact even exist? How did she know He existed? Had she ever personally seen Him do anything? There had been other tests in her lifetime, but how could you know the results were right—as they certainly were not in her case? The only real miracles she could think of had happened long ago—turning the Nile into blood, parting the Red Sea, making bread fall from heaven. But how could she know these things had actually happened? Were they just fables thought up by the priests so they could do no work but live off the tithes and offerings of people like herself? Had her people's possession of their land indeed been so miraculous? They had lost some battles, at Ai for instance, although the priests had an excuse for that. There was always an excuse why miracles didn't work, always a reason. What reason could the priests postulate in her case? She was guilty, and Yahweh and the test He had provided had failed to perceive it. Yahweh had failed to prove her guilt—or even His existence.

The more she thought about it, the more convinced she became. For Yahweh's "chosen people," they certainly had a lot of problems. Why were the nations around them still invading and oppressing them? Either Yahweh was weaker than those nations' gods (a possibility the priests vehemently denied) or He didn't exist at all. In either case, He was not worthy of respect. What other possibility could there be? If she had begun her reasoning from the existence of an all-powerful Yahweh, what possible conclusion could she have reached? She could see none. If Yahweh did not exist, then she must turn her thinking to what did exist, her own situation.

*****

That day, Hannah returned to her work, checking on her small garden, gathering the produce that was ripe, grinding grain, fetching water, cooking, washing clothes. It felt mechanical and forced, unimportant, even unreal perhaps. The normal routine did not seem normal, but she did it that day—and the next day and the next day and the days after that.

Things returned to normal with her husband as well, even possibly better somehow. They resumed marital relations, which also seemed different. He was more attentive, more aware of her, as if he saw her differently now.

She had less reason to seek love elsewhere. And, having luckily escaped once, she was not anxious to risk all again. It was not that she feared the priest's test. That was a dead issue. But she did fear being caught by her husband, or someone else. Mostly, she was afraid of upsetting her new-found tranquility.

As the days went by, she thought more and more about her situation. She had certainly been lucky, first to escape detection and then to survive the test. Some did not, she knew. She had heard of other unfaithful wives suffering slowly and painfully after the test and eventually being divorced by their husbands. These were stories told by older women, not by the priests, so she knew they were true. The older women had actually known these women. Why had she been lucky enough to escape that? Had the guilt of some women been so strong that they had made themselves sick thinking about it? Or was it that the temple dirt had naturally made some women sick and not others? What if there was some natural contamination in the dirt that some had received? What if it was just accident or chance that had made some women sick and not others?

The question intrigued her. Why had she been one of the lucky ones? Did she deserve this for some reason? She knew she was guilty. What if Yahweh had really been there and had known of her guilt but had chosen not to speak through the test? She had known and not spoken. The young man who had been her lover had known and not spoken. Could Yahweh also have known but not spoken? But why? Why would He do that?

*****

The days went by as Hannah continued with her duties, grinding grain, cooking, cleaning, weaving. It was six or seven months after the test that she first noticed a very slight swelling in her belly. She didn't believe it. Not that first week. Nor the next week. By the third week, it could not be denied. She said nothing. It was another month before Eliakim noticed. He also said nothing, but the same mix of emotions—hurt, anger, worry, and concern—was evident on his face, as evident as the swelling of her belly.

Weeks passed in silent stress. Husband and wife barely spoke. Chores were done without thinking. Some were forgotten, some neglected.

The first sensation of movement confused her. She did not understand. The movements continued from time to time and strengthened. One day, she took her husband's hand and guided it to her belly. He started to pull his hand away in anger, but stopped, his face twisted in confusion and then wonder.

The baby was born four months later. When the midwife placed the child in her arms, she stared down at him in wonder and gratitude. What had she done to deserve this redemption in place of the expected condemnation? She stared in speechless gratitude at the son who had vindicated her.

*****

Eight days later, the boy was taken to the priest to be circumcised. Hannah and Eliakim named him Yeshua. On the fortieth day, Hannah brought to the priest at the entrance of the tabernacle a lamb a year old for a burnt offering and a pigeon for a sin offering. It was the same priest who had administered the oath and the test, but he did not acknowledge her previous appearance, solemnly accepting the offering and granting her the blessing.

Hannah began to take an interest in the religious ceremonies. With a renewed understanding, she prepared the unleavened cakes and the Passover lamb. As she worked, she hummed to herself the Passover hymns. She ate the meal with Eliakim, with the baby in a cradle beside her, and her heart swelled with wonder and amazement at the thought that she was having her own Passover experience.

She felt indeed that the avenging angel had passed over her. The innocent lamb had died, and she had been granted life.

She felt with a certainty that she could not explain that the stories were true, that Yahweh had indeed saved her people from slavery in Egypt. She knew that it was Yahweh, not Moses, who had parted the Red Sea. She understood as well that the slaves in Egypt had not been rescued because they deserved it. They had not been saved because of their righteousness but because of Yahweh's mercy. She understood this because she, too, had been spared, not because of her righteousness, but because of Yahweh's mercy.

Hannah wondered, too, about her husband Eliakim, whose name meant "God establishes." Did he also have a new understanding? She sensed in him a renewed reverence. In him, it was explicable. The test had worked, vindicating the righteous. He thought of her, his wife, as pure and righteous.

But she knew differently. How could the inexplicable be explained for her? She now knew with certainty that Yahweh had not been fooled. He had known all along what she had done. The test had been designed to reveal the truth—not to Yahweh and not to her husband—but to her. Yahweh had known the truth even before the test, and yet, and yet, she had been spared. Why would the holy God do this?

In the presence of the holy God, she knew with certainty that she was guilty. Her sin was known, her sinfulness was real. And yet somehow her sin had been covered. In awe, she felt greatly blessed—and somehow, inexplicably, forgiven.

"Amen. So be it" (Numbers 5:22).

The Puritan and The Last Strumpet

When the Puritans came to the new world, they saw it as a place where the creation had not been defiled and degraded, a place to which the Kingdom of God could come on earth in perfection.

Nevertheless, there soon moved in among them an evil lot, sinners and adulterers and idolaters and profane men and women. These men and women had to be rounded up and kept from contaminating the purity of the new flock. And so there developed a prison in the seaport of New Purity, a house where convicted offenders were kept for a time. The serious offenders were then sold into slavery to a plantation owner in the lower states.

There was in this house one day a lone woman, young enough to still be attractive yet debauched enough to look a little worn and decaying around the face. Alone, she sat on the straw on the floor of a large room in the basement. The only light came through a small window with bars in the locked door.

To this place came a short, stumpy man in a black hat and black suit. His complexion was swarthy, and his hands were gnarled. Yet, he retained the power and energy of youth, being, one would suppose from his appearance, in his early thirties. He approached the proprietor of the establishment.

"Hast thou any women in thy gaol this day?" he asked.

The proprietor looked over the inquirer. "We have only one left at the moment—a strumpet, guilty of theft and whatever other crimes one would learn on the streets."

The Puritan—for this is what the short, stocky man was—asked to see her. He looked through the bars to where she sat, fingering her bodice sullenly, defiantly.

"What is thy name?" he inquired.

"Rahab," she replied.

"A fitting name for a strumpet," he said. "I will take her."

The Puritan paid the proprietor the stated price and bought the strumpet, who was for sale as a slave. He took the keys from the proprietor and unlocked the barred door. Then, he took the strumpet's hand in his powerful grip and led her outside to where a wagon was waiting. He helped her climb up to the seat and then climbed up beside her. They drove through the seaport to a quieter lane and stopped before a dressmaker's shop. The Puritan helped his charge down from the wagon and led her inside.

"Miss Prudence," he said to the manager of the shop, "I want thee to supply a complete outfit of clothes for this young woman, including some sort of attire for sleeping in. She needn't put the clothes on here. We can take them in a box."

The Puritan then went next door to the hardware shop, leaving Miss Prudence to measure up the strumpet.

"Do you know that man?" the strumpet asked when he had gone. "What kind of man is he?"

"He is a Puritan," replied Miss Prudence.

"What kind of a Puritan?"

"Just a Puritan. They are all alike."

In a few minutes, the Puritan returned, and they went off with the box of clothes. After a half-hour, the wagon stopped in front of a small house on a country lane. With his powerful grip on the strumpet's hand, the Puritan led her inside.

"This is the front hall, and this is the parlour," he said.

The rooms were well furnished, neat yet comfortable. The furniture was solid oak.

"I am not a good housekeeper," the strumpet said sullenly.

"Thou wilt learn," the Puritan replied. "This is the kitchen, and this is the pantry."

"I cannot cook," the strumpet said defiantly.

"Thou wilt learn. This is the upstairs," the Puritan said, indicating the staircase, and he led her upstairs. "This is the master bedroom, and these two are guest rooms."

"And which one will I sleep in?" she demanded.

"The master bedroom."

"And you a good Puritan? Do you sleep with all of your servants? What happened to your last servant? Is she in childbed somewhere?"

"I have never had a servant in my life."

"Then why did you buy me for a servant?"

"I did not buy thee for a servant. I bought thee to be my wife. If thou wilt agree, we shall go over to the parson's house and be married this afternoon."

*****

The next day, the strumpet—or the wife, for such she was now—began to learn to cook and clean, with the help of an old housewife the master had asked to come in and teach her. She wore her new clothes now and at night the flannel nightgown the master had bought her. To her surprise, he proved to be inexperienced yet sure, kind, and sensitive. She had never encountered anything like that in her life before this.

After a few days, the master rose one morning, put on his best suit, and announced, "'Tis Sunday. We shall be going to church. Dress in thy good clothes, and comb thy hair. When we go into the church, sit quietly, do as the others do, and do not say anything."

The church was a small, white frame building. Around it were other wagons and buggies and other Puritans in black hats and coats and other women in long, modest dresses and sunbonnets and children dressed like miniature Puritans and wives, trailing respectfully and obediently behind their elders.

They entered the building. The Puritan removed his hat, directed her to the side where the women and children sat, and then walked over to sit down among the men. A couple of ladies moved over and made room for her on the end of a bench and smiled politely.

She spent most of the service with her head down, not daring to look around or speak, peeking out of the corner of her eye at these strange men in their black suits and these prim and proper ladies. She did not understand much of what was said but kept sneaking glimpses of these strange men and equally strange women and children.

*****

The strumpet wife learned to cook, and she learned to keep house, and she learned to sew.

One day, the master went out of the house and left his purse sitting on the table. Her old habits returned to her. Quickly, she took the purse, emptied out the coins, and slipped them into the pocket of her dress. Turning, she saw the master silhouetted in the doorway, with his arms stretched out against the doorposts.

"Why art thou doing that?" he asked. "Thou dost not have to steal the money. Indeed, thou canst not steal it. Thou ownst it. It is thine."

He turned and walked away.

*****

Another day, the master was away to town on business. Seeing her chance, she threw her cloak about her shoulders, slipped out the door, and ran down the road. Coming to a crossroad, she turned and went a way along another road. She ran and stumbled for hours, until she was exhausted and very hungry.

Toward evening, a wagon rumbled down the road behind her. It was the master. He helped her climb up into the wagon.

"Why didst thou run away?" he asked.

"Because I saw you were away and I had a chance to escape without you holding me there."

"There is no restraint to hold thee there. Thou canst leave at any time, whether I be present or not."

"But if I tried to run away when you were there, you would become angry with me and put me back into slavery."

"Thou wouldst indeed go back into slavery, but I would not put thee there. Thou wouldst do it thyself. Where else couldst thou go? How else wouldst thou live? Thou wouldst of necessity turn back to thy former ways, wouldst be caught and convicted, and wouldst again be put into bonds to be sold into slavery."

*****

One other day when the master was away, she saw a young man walking by the house. He was pleasing to look at. Remembering her former ways, she enticed him to come onto the porch. Fearing the master, she led him into the nearby woods, and they lay together. However, what began as anticipated pleasure ended with a burning pain. Confused, she stared into the young man's red eyes. When they were finished, she rose and walked to the edge of the woods. The master was waiting for her there. He took her again by the hand in his strong grip and led her back to the house. He took her up the stairs and into the bedroom and lay with her there. It was pleasant, comforting, and reassuring.

*****

Another day, when the work was all done and they were sitting in the parlor before the fire, Rahab asked her husband, "Why did you marry me?"

"I chose thee."

"Yes, but why did you choose me? Surely there were Puritan women you could have married."

96

"Yes, I suppose so. Yet, most of the Puritan women want tall, good-looking husbands. There was nothing in my appearance that women would desire me. But yes, there were some of them I could have married, and might have."

"Then why did you marry me?" she insisted.

"It is written," he replied, "that the one who is forgiven little loves little, but the one who is forgiven much loves much. I believed that thou hadst the potential to be a good wife."

*****

A year and a half later, she produced her first child. She smiled, beaming, into her husband's face. She was sure she had done something now to make herself worthy of her husband. He was pleased, but he loved her just the same. After all, it was his child, begotten in her by himself.

"Husbands, love your wives, just as Christ loved the church and gave himself up for her to make her holy...and to present her to himself as a radiant church, without stain or wrinkle or any other blemish, but holy and blameless...This is a profound mystery—but I am talking about Christ and the church"
(Ephesians 5:25-32).

The Advocate

"The case that I have presented contains the most definitive and most convincing compilation of evidence I have ever seen in my career," the Prosecutor said. "The defendant, Adam Mann, has committed a horrendous string of crimes—robberies, assaults, frauds, and murders. You have heard from a hundred and eighty-two eyewitnesses of his crimes who know Adam Mann well and who saw and testified to what he did. Many of his crimes were caught on videotape. You have heard audio tapes of Mr. Mann admitting to many of his crimes. Mr. Mann left his fingerprints on multiple weapons at many crime scenes. His DNA was found on twelve different victims. He was caught red-handed in possession of various weapons used in the commission of his crimes and in possession of many of the items he has been accused of stealing. His Advocate has not been able to mount any defence to these charges. The evidence is absolutely overwhelming. There is no possible verdict other than to find Adam Mann guilty. I rest my case."

The Judge turned to the defence table. "Is there anything that can be said in defence of Mr. Mann? Do you have anything to say?"

Adam Mann leaned over and spoke quietly to his Advocate. "You have heard the evidence. I admit it. I'm guilty. I am going to be executed, and I deserve it. What could you possibly say that would make any difference?"

The Advocate reached over and gently patted his client on the arm. "Don't worry," he said. "Don't be afraid."

Then the Advocate stood and approached the Judge. A large file was in his hand. He placed the file in front of the judge. "Your Honor, I would like to place into evidence a transcript of case number 1189 from the Imperial Supreme Court. The transcript states that a man named Joshua King has already been convicted of every one of the charges now levied against Adam Mann. Furthermore, Joshua King was executed for these crimes three years ago."

The Prosecutor jumped to his feet. "Your Honor, this is preposterous," he said. "Joshua King is clearly innocent of these crimes. The evidence conclusively proves that Adam Mann is guilty of them."

"That may be," the Advocate responded, "but the penalty for these crimes has already been paid. The penalty cannot be paid twice. That would be unjust."

The Judge pulled the massive file toward him and skimmed through it, stopping on the final page. He breathed deeply. "Will the defendant please stand."

Adam Mann stood. His Advocate stood at his side, his arm across Adam's shoulders.

"Mr. Mann," the Judge stated, "a decision by the Imperial Supreme Court is final. It cannot be challenged. Joshua King has pled guilty to every one of the crimes with which you have been charged, and he has paid for them by allowing himself to be executed. Therefore, this court has no option but to declare you not guilty on all of the charges brought against you. You are free to go."

Stunned, Adam Mann thanked his Advocate and turned to leave.

As he turned, Mann was surprised to see that the Judge had come down off the bench. He put a hand on Mann's shoulder, "You are free. Now go. You are no longer guilty. You are no longer bound. You are free to go and commit no more crimes. You are free to go into all the world. I have set you free, and you are really free. You are free."

Daddy's Ghost

The twelve children stood in silence around the bed. Their father was propped up on pillows. He looked around at them all.

"I appreciate all of you for coming," he said.

"Well, of course," James said. "We love you."

The father took a deep breath and released it. "It is time," he said. "Time for me to go."

"But how will we manage without you?" Peter asked.

"You have important jobs, you have responsibilities, and you are scattered all over the world. You do not see me for months on end. How can I be present with all of you at the same time?"

They all raised objections, one after another.

"Enough! Peace," he said. "It will be better for you this way."

"How could it be better?" Peter demanded. "We need you."

*****

At the end of the week, their father died. They cried and mourned and grieved. The next few days were a blur as they arranged the funeral and took care of all of the other details. And then they scattered, back to their lives.

*****

"Hi, John. It's Mary. How are you doing?"

"Pretty good, actually. How are you?"

"Doing good. Feeling better. Something strange happened. You know I've been feeling down lately. But last night I had a dream. I was standing on a cliff in the middle of a storm, and then suddenly Dad was there. He put his arms around me and just held me there. It felt incredibly comforting. We just stood there for a long time, and when I finally looked up, we were standing in a beautiful, green valley with a little stream running through it. It was just a dream, but when I woke up this morning, I still felt the same way. I felt comforted and safe. The feeling has stayed with me all day. I had a very good day. I know it sounds silly."

"Not so silly, actually. Something happened to me too. I had a very complex problem at work. I wasn't sure what to do. And then I remembered something Dad had told us: 'You can't have two bosses.' I could hear him saying the words. And he was right. I knew exactly what I had to do."

*****

Hi, James. Sorry for the email. Something rather strange happened to me today. I had to make a presentation, a talk really, defending what I was doing. I had no time to prepare, and I didn't know what to say. But when the time came, it was as if Dad was standing right beside me, whispering the words into my ear as I was speaking them. They were the right words. It went well.

Andrew

*****

To my brothers and sisters:

Here is an update on my situation. I have continued my investigations and am learning more and more every day. I seem to be guided into discovering new things, making new connections, deepening my understanding. It is as if there is a secret path that I don't know but someone who does know is leading me through the darkness to light.

Paul

101

*****

Dear brothers and sisters,

I am writing to tell you I have decided to testify. Bad men have threatened to kill me if I do, but I must tell what I know. I must tell the truth.

It has been a hard decision. Frankly, I am terrified.

What made me decide to do this?

I went for a hike in the mountains. I was sitting beside a lake when I heard thunder out of a clear sky. It seemed to be speaking my name. And then these words were there in my mind, not spoken, not written, but very clear: "Do not be afraid. I am with you. Be brave, and do the right thing."

Was it Dad? I don't know. But I know he would have been pleased with my decision.

Stephen

*****

Dear brothers and sisters:

I am writing to tell you that our son Malcolm has come home. As you know, we have not seen him for three years. We did not know where he was.

He just appeared on our doorstep. He said he was sorry for what he had done to Elizabeth and me. He broke down in tears. We hugged him.

After a time, we asked him what had led him to come back. He said he had completed some scheme and was feeling pretty satisfied with himself but not quite at ease either. Then, a great fear came over him. He heard a disembodied voice speaking in his ear, "What you are doing, the way you are living, is wrong. You need to change."

We do not understand it, but Elizabeth and I are very grateful.

Your brother,
Timothy

*****

And so on and so on and so on and so on and so on and so on and so on...

Victor

Victor was born in a land devastated by war and corruption. He grew up in poverty and deprivation in an orphanage. There was no one who loved him, and his future looked bleak, offering little in the way of education or employment. He was alive, but just barely. He could not be said to be living, merely existing. He had no purpose, did not matter to anyone, would most likely never amount to anything or make a difference in the world. Deep down, Victor had a sense that this was not the way things should be. He had heard rumors that not all children lived this way, that some children lived in a good house, had a father and mother, ate good food, slept in a soft bed, had new toys to play with, and went to good schools where they made good friends and learned many new things. He felt cheated. He was angry a lot of the time, taking out his frustration on the children around him, taking their toys and hitting, kicking, and biting them when he thought the orphanage workers were not watching. But they did see him sometimes, and then they punished him severely and told him that he was a bad boy who deserved to live in an orphanage for the rest of his life.

One day, an average-looking man came. He walked through the orphanage, making his way between the hard metal cots of the dormitory and across the worn linoleum floor where the children were trying to play with a few broken toys. He smiled at the children and watched them play. Once, he stooped down and made a few minor adjustments to fix one of the toys.

After a while, he walked over to where Victor was sitting in a corner by himself. He squatted down in front of

Victor, smiled, and held out his hand. "Good morning, Victor," he said.

But Victor did not take the man's hand, and he did not smile. He did not trust this stranger. He did not trust any adults, nor any children either. He turned his little body and face away from the stranger, but he kept an eye on the stranger over his shoulder.

The man smiled, got up, and walked away.

The next day, he was back. He did the same things as before, walking around the orphanage, looking at the miserable beds, broken toys, and peeling walls, and watching the children play. He smiled again at Victor, this time from across the room, but Victor again turned his face away.

On the third day, Victor did not see the man all morning. At noon, he was sitting at a table by himself when a shadow fell over the thin soup and stale bun in front of him. Startled, he looked up. The strange man was sitting down across the table from him. He smiled at Victor. Victor saw that he had a bowl of the orphanage soup and a stale bun. He began eating the soup, but then he did a strange thing. He took his stale bun, broke it in half, and put one half on Victor's plate. Then, he took his glass of fruit juice and poured some into Victor's glass, filling it up to the brim. Then, he resumed eating. Victor did not know what to say or do, so he just kept eating, finishing his own food, as well as the half-bun the stranger had given him, and drinking all the juice.

When they both had finished eating, the man stood up, picked up all of the dirty dishes, smiled at Victor, and walked toward the kitchen.

Victor went back to the playroom, where he sat in a corner, not doing much of anything. None of the other children ever played with him anyway. He sat there for two hours, until his head had begun to droop with fatigue and boredom.

A large hand, placed gently on his head, startled him awake.

"Hello, Victor." The strange man smiled down at him. Then, in a movement so swift that Victor did not see it coming, he bent down and scooped Victor up into his arms.

Victor was so frightened that he could not speak or call out, and he would not have done so anyway because he did not believe that there was anyone at the orphanage who cared enough about him to rescue him from this stranger.

The stranger carried Victor to the far end of the room, where there was a large, stuffed chair with sagging springs and stuffing coming out through holes in four different places. The stranger sat down on the chair, settled Victor on his knee, and smiled again.

Victor did not know what to say or do, so he just stared at the stranger.

The stranger smiled again, then began speaking. He had a deep, clear voice. "Once upon a time," he began, "things were not as they are now…"

For the next hour, the man told stories to Victor, and the time seemed to fly by. They were fascinating stories. Stories about loss and pain and how things were not the way they were supposed to be. Stories about how things could be, how people ought to live, stories about love and peace and giving and joy and purpose. And stories about another country, the country the stranger came from. It was a place that Victor had always dreamed was possible, where children lived in a good house, had their own father and mother, ate as much good food as they wanted, slept in a soft bed, had new toys and good friends, and went to school.

Victor imagined what it would be like to live in that country, what it would be like if *he* were to live in that country. It was like a dream, and when he awoke, it was suppertime, and he was curled up alone in the big chair.

The next day, Victor woke up wondering what would happen that day. For the first time that he could remember, he did not start the day angry. But he did not see the stranger all morning, nor at lunchtime. After lunch, he sat down in his corner again and hung his head. Perhaps it had all been a dream.

But then he felt a familiar touch on his forehead, and he looked up into the eyes of the stranger. The man reached down as before, picked Victor up, and carried him to the big chair. Again, the stranger told him stories, stories of being lost and being found, of being alone and being loved, of evil and goodness, stories of the past and stories of the future, and, above all, stories of the wonderful country the stranger came from.

This time, Victor did not fall asleep. But, after an hour or two, the man got up and put Victor gently down on the big chair. They did not say goodbye, and Victor scarcely saw the man go. He just sat there in the big chair, feeling warm and happy and loved.

The man did not come the next day, but he came the day after that and again told Victor stories sitting in the chair. In addition to the other stories, he told Victor about the house he himself lived in, in the country far away. It was a big, beautiful, comfortable house with many bedrooms. He told Victor about his wife and his children, two girls and a boy, all about Victor's age.

Life went on like this for three weeks. Some days, the man came and told Victor stories or played with him or just walked around the dreary orphanage holding him in his arms. Some days, he did not come at all.

The stranger had been gone for two days, and Victor was starting to worry that the stranger had gone back to his own country and he would not see him again. But, on the third day, the stranger appeared. He had a serious look on his face. He went over to where Victor was sitting in the middle of the floor, smiled, bent down, and picked him up as before.

This time, he did not take Victor to the big chair. Instead, he carried Victor down a long, dark hall to the office of Miss Djamenor, the administrator of the orphanage. He knocked on the door, walked in, and set Victor down in a chair in front of the desk where the administrator was sitting. Then, he himself sat down in another chair beside Victor.

"This is Mr. Theamor," the administrator said to Victor and then paused. Victor said nothing, so she continued. "He has applied to adopt you. He says he wants to be your father."

Victor was dumbfounded. He did not know what to say. He just sat and stared at the administrator, afraid to look at the stranger.

"Do you understand, Victor?"

He nodded.

"Now, Victor, if Mr. Theamor adopts you, this will be final. You can never be adopted by anyone else. Furthermore, if you are adopted by this man, you will no longer live here in this orphanage or even in this country. Mr. Theamor is not from here. He comes from another country. If he adopts you, you will have to go away with him and live in his country. You will never be able to come back. You will no longer be a citizen of this country but will be a citizen of that country. That is a country far away from here, and they speak a completely different language there. You will not understand what people are saying, and they will not understand you. Do you understand this?"

Victor nodded again.

"This is a very big decision," the administrator continued. "You do not have to be adopted by Mr. Theamor. You do not have to go with him or go to his country. You can stay here in this country and live in this orphanage. The decision will be up to you. As I said, this is a big decision, and you may want to take some time to think about it. I suggest you think about it for a few days, and when you have made your mind up, you can ask to come and see me. Alright, Victor?"

Victor stared at her. Then, he turned and slowly looked up at the face of the stranger. Mr. Theamor looked gently down at the boy but did not speak.

"No," the boy said.

The administrator sighed. "You mean you do not want to be adopted by this man? You do not want to become his son and move to his country?"

"No," Victor said. "I mean I do not want to wait. I want to be adopted by Mr. Theamor and be his son and go to live in his country."

"Are you sure, Victor?" the woman asked. "You do not have to make a decision now. Mr. Theamor will not withdraw his offer. You can still decide later to accept it."

"I am sure," Victor responded. "I want to be adopted now."

"Very well," the administrator said. She pulled a piece of paper out of a file folder. She placed it on her desk in front of Victor. "These are the adoption papers. Can you write your name, Victor?"

The boy nodded.

"Good. This paper says that you want to be adopted by Mr. Theamor, that you want to be his son. If you want to do that, please write your name here at the bottom." She held a pen out to him.

The boy solemnly took the pen and painstakingly, a letter at a time, printed his name at the bottom of the paper.

"Now, this paper says that you are giving up your right to citizenship in this country and are applying to be a citizen of Mr. Theamor's country. Are you sure you want to do this?"

Without speaking, the boy leaned forward and printed his name at the bottom of the second piece of paper too. When he had finished, he looked up at the administrator and slowly turned to the stranger beside him who had become his father.

"That is all we need to do," Miss Djamenor said. "Now, Victor, the law says that no adoption will become final until forty days after the papers are signed. You will remain living here in the orphanage for that time. If you change your mind, ask to come and see me, and we can tear up these papers. If we do that, you will not have to be adopted by Mr.

Theamor, and you will not have to move to his country. Do you understand?"

The boy nodded.

"If, forty days from now, you still wish to be adopted, Mr. Theamor will return then and take you with him to his country."

Again, Victor nodded.

The man stood up, bent down, and scooped Victor up in his arms. "I love you, Victor," he said. "I am so glad that you want to be my son. I am glad that I am going to be your father." He hugged Victor tightly in his arms, and tears of joy began trickling down the boy's face. "I must go now," the man continued. "I will come back and get you in forty days."

The boy nodded, smiled, and gulped as the man put him gently back in the chair. The man shook hands with the administrator, turned, and walked out through the door.

After a moment, the administrator said, "You may go now, Victor. Go out the door, and go down the hall to your right until you come to the other hall that leads to the play area."

The boy slid off the chair and silently left the room.

Back in the play area, the boy sat on the floor in the corner of the room, thinking and looking at the other children playing.

The next morning, Victor got up as usual. He made his bed with care and then tidied up the floor around the bed. After breakfast, he went to the play area as usual and sat in his corner, looking at the other children. After a while, he crawled over to where two younger children were sitting and started to play with them, shyly at first, then gradually becoming more comfortable. He touched one boy on the shoulder and smiled at him.

At lunchtime, Victor sat with some other children. Seeing the sad look on one little boy's face, Victor broke a small chunk off his own stale bun and handed it to the smaller boy.

That night, just before bedtime, the stranger appeared again. He picked Victor up, carried him to his bed, put Victor down, and sat down beside him. Then, he picked up a big bag he had set next to the bed and handed it to Victor.

Victor looked at him wonderingly, then opened the bag. Inside was a big, brown teddy bear with wonderfully kind, wise eyes.

"His name is Chokmah," the man said. "He can be with you to remind you of me when I'm not here."

When he awoke the next day, Victor lay on his bed, his teddy bear in his arm, looking at the ceiling. "I have a name," he said to himself. "I am Victor Theamor. I have a father who loves me, and I am going to go and live in a wonderful country."

That day, Victor not only made his own bed, but also helped two other children make theirs. Then he got a broom and swept the floor of the whole dormitory room. That morning, he played with other children, smiling at them, sharing toys, and even giving one a hug when he fell and hurt his knee.

One afternoon a couple of days later, Victor felt especially brave. He picked up one little boy that he especially had grown to like and carried him over to the big chair. With a great effort, he hoisted the other boy up into the chair and then crawled up after him. Then, he began to tell the other boy stories, stories of pain and loss, stories of love and hope, stories of a wonderful land where boys and girls were loved and cared for, the stories that the strange man had told him.

Some of the older boys and girls made fun of Victor for believing the stories that the strange man had told him. Sometimes, they hit him or kicked him or took his toys when no one was looking. A couple of times, Victor became angry and hit back, but mostly he just ignored them and kept on doing what he had been doing.

His father visited him a few times, sometimes bringing a small present and sometimes telling him more stories and once just giving him a long, gentle hug. Many days, he did not come at all. One day, he did not come, but there was a wrapped package lying on Victor's bed at bedtime. He opened it up. It was a battery-powered tape recorder. Victor had never seen such a thing before, but he pushed the "play" button and was startled to hear the man's voice telling his stories.

And so, the days passed. Victor helped keep his area of the orphanage clean and tidy. He played with the younger children, giving them toys and smiles and hugs. Every afternoon, he gathered a group of children around him and told them the stories his father had told him.

One day, Miss Djamenor stood in the doorway of the play area watching Victor and the other children.

"Victor, please come here," she said.

The boy obediently walked over and stood in front of the woman.

"Victor," she said, "do you really think Mr. Theamor is going to come back for you?"

The boy looked up at her, a troubled look on his face. He thought a moment and then said, "Yes, I do."

"Why do you think that, Victor?"

"Because I think he loves me," the boy replied. "He is a good, honest man, and he promised he would come back."

"And are you convinced he is going to take you to live with him in his country?"

"Yes," the boy replied.

"But how do you know there even is such a country?"

"There must be such a country," the boy replied, "because I am a citizen of it."

"But how do you know it exists? You've never been there. You've never seen it. You don't even speak the right language. And if it does exist, how do you know it will be as Mr. Theamor says it is? How do you know it is a wonderful place? Mr. Theamor has brought you only a few small presents. How do you know there will be all those good things there that he told you about? How do you know that you will even like it there?"

The boy thought about this for a moment. "It is true that I have never seen that country," he said, "even though I am a citizen of it. I do not really know that country, but I have gotten to know my father. He is a very good man, and I know he loves me. If he says his country is a wonderful place, then I am sure it must be. And he will be there. He has made this old orphanage a nicer place, and if he is in that country, that must be a nice place too. I am not going there so much because I want to be in that country but because I want to be with my father. I trust my father."

Higher Power

Alexander Tomkins was miffed. Not really angry. Just a little miffed. He was about to be interviewed for a senior position with Hodgson, Hodgson, and Hughes, and they had asked him to wait down here in the first-floor lobby of the bank tower. Of course, it was Saturday morning, and they had explained that new carpets were being installed in their reception area on the fourteenth floor. But they had known about both the interview and the carpet laying ahead of time, and they could have arranged to meet somewhere else.

It was a bit troubling, but Alexander tried to put the matter in perspective. He was still in line for that attractive position, and it would not do to get agitated. He settled down to wait on one of the two padded bench seats by the elevators, the only one of the two that had been vacant. They had told him that they were running a bit late and they would come down and get him within twenty minutes.

Alexander glanced at the newspaper that someone had left on the seat, and then across at the other seat. There was a man there, his shoes off, his head resting on a brown knapsack and his knees curled up in fetal position. He was grunting audibly as if in hope that someone would notice him.

Alexander looked back at the newspaper. The man opposite grunted again and sat up, rubbing at his bleary eyes. He groaned and looked across at Alexander. "Six months," he said.

"What?" Alexander answered, startled into making a reply.

"Women and whiskey," the other said.

Alexander stared at him without saying anything further. Apparently, the man was given to speaking in phrases that didn't follow each other in any logical way.

"Too much women and whiskey," the man said again. "I didn't have enough will power to resist."

Alexander nodded.

"My sister has a good job as a nurse in Williams Lake," the man continued. "She's very successful and a good woman. She won't talk to me until I have been sober for a year."

"She probably wants what's best for you," Alexander said. "That's tough love. She's giving you a good reason to stop drinking."

"What's your name?"

"Alexander Tomkins."

A young woman in a well-cut business suit came in through the street door and walked between the two men to the elevators. The door opened immediately, and she went up.

"Beauty of creation attracts us." The man leered. "Nice, eh?"

Tomkins had barely noticed the woman.

"You a businessman?"

"Close enough."

The man struggled to his feet, walked with a stiff-legged limp over to the bench where Alexander was, and sat down on the newspaper next to him. He pulled on one of the shoes he was carrying, took the laces out of the top hole, and then pushed a loop back through. He then took the lace ends, threaded them through the loops on the opposite sides and pulled them tight. "Then you cut off the ends. You got kids?" he asked.

"Yes."

"Play sports?"

"My daughter plays soccer."

"Tie your shoes like this. They never come loose, and no knot in front to hurt your foot."

"Ah. That's quite clever."

"I gotta go back to church and straighten out my life."

"That would be a good idea."

"Mr. Tomkins, sir, it normally costs a lot. This woman gave me training for free in the park. Stretching and pushing. Think it'll help?"

"I don't know."

"That gallon fong thing."

"Oh. Probably not."

"She said it unleashes the power inside you?"

"Oh." Alexander paused. "What's inside you?"

"Sorry, Mr. Tomkins, sir." The man got up and limped back to the other bench. "I smell."

Alexander hadn't noticed any smell.

"I told him not to do drugs. They mess you up. I never did it. I only tried a couple times."

The man was sitting on the bench again. His thick head of fair hair was turning gray, but Alexander could see that he must have been a handsome man once.

"Sober six months. I gotta get sober again."

Alexander held up his left hand. "I was given this watch twenty-five years ago. A man in my church said he would give a gold watch to any of the kids in the church who would promise not to drink or smoke or take drugs. If they kept the promise until they were twenty-one, they got the watch. However, they had to promise not to drink or smoke or take drugs, not just until twenty-one but for their whole life."

"Must be valuable, Mr. Tomkins, sir," the man said, eyeing the gold band.

"No, not now. But I have a compulsive personality. If I had ever started drinking, I would probably have become an alcoholic."

"Watch saved you, eh?"

"It wasn't really the watch. I lost the watch once, for five months—but I didn't start drinking."

"Lost?"

"I found it again five months later. It had fallen behind a drawer.

"I lost..."

The other man, seeming to forget what he had started to say, busied himself with his backpack for a while, pulling out a cleaner shirt and socks. He limped around the corner behind the elevators and came back wearing the other clothes. He looked down into the knapsack. "It's empty inside."

He rummaged in the knapsack some more and pulled out two hats, a baseball cap and a cloth sun hat, and put both on his head. "Helicopter logger. Tough work. I was one of the best. I grew up in logging camps. Everyone drank. There were a lot of good ones. The others are all dead. That's not like being a businessman, Mr. Tomkins, sir. That must be great."

Alexander shrugged his narrow shoulders. "I could never make a living as a logger. Some people are good at one thing, others at another. You do what you're good at. There's nothing wrong with being a logger."

"We had a house in '90. Paid forty thousand, and in five years it was worth a hundred and eight. My lady was playing around."

"I'm sorry to hear that."

"My mother died, my brothers and sister wouldn't give me nothing. Lost the house."

Alexander nodded.

"Maybe somebody'll make me a coach again. Used to coach minor league soccer, hockey. I'm forty-eight. I don't care about material things."

Alexander wasn't sure about the logical connections between these statements. He also couldn't see anyone allowing this man near children.

"Two days ago, my younger brother died. Overdose of cocaine. He was thirty-eight. Got drunk to say goodbye. I handle stuff that way. Can't stop it."

Alexander nodded. "That's not a good way to handle things."

"They say a light bulb or a tree, it don't matter. I don't think so."

"A light bulb or tree?"

"Your higher power. They say it can be a light bulb or tree or anything. It don't make sense."

"You're right. A light bulb doesn't have any power. It can't help you."

"I need God," the man said.

The elevator doors jerked open, and a middle-aged woman in a neat business suit came out. "Mr. Tomkins?"

He stood, walked across to the other bench, and put his hand on the other man's shoulder. "I hope you make it," he said.

"I hope you make it too, Mr. Tomkins, sir."

Alexander smiled. "Thank you."

The woman in the business suit looked at Alexander suspiciously.

Alexander entered the elevator, looked back at the man on the bench, and smiled. He glanced over at the trim woman beside him, then at his wristwatch, and then back at the man on the bench. "A higher power makes the difference. I'll pray you'll make it," he said as the elevator doors closed.

Midtown Bus

The midtown bus lurched along, carrying its random assortment of humanity.

"Someone should do something," muttered the old woman, squeezed between two middle-aged businessmen on the seniors' bench near the front.

The driver, balding with a spreading middle, hunched over the wheel, his eyes on the road, his ears closed to what was happening behind him.

A line of swaying passengers, dangling from hand straps, stretched halfway down the aisle.

A thirty-something man with tattoos on his bulging arms sat stoically on an outside seat, no one daring to squeeze past him to the empty inside seat.

In the back, a half-dozen older teens in jeans and black T-shirts lounged on the benches.

"Hey, Paki! What you doing on our bus? Why don't you go back to India where you belong?" one of them called.

Their target was a wiry, middle-aged Latino with a brown face and black hair, last in the line of swaying standees. He kept his face down, staring at the floor.

"Hey, babe! Want to come back here and give us some honey?"

Their target had switched to a young woman in a black skirt and a white sweater. She glanced up, horrified, then turned her face away to stare at the back door.

Two burly men in a middle seat glanced back at the commotion, then turned up the volume for the music on their iPhones.

"Paki, when you get off this bus, we're going to stick you real good. You should've stayed where you belong."

"Somebody should do something," muttered the old lady again, perhaps a repetitive phrase inspired by burgeoning dementia.

The bus lurched to a stop to let on one more passenger, a middle-aged woman in a wrinkled business suit. She joined the line of standees.

In the pause, an old man near the back doors slowly pulled himself to his feet, leaning heavily on a wooden cane. He lurched out of the row into the swaying line. He looked into the face of a dowdy, middle-aged woman in green slacks, who had turned to check on the movement behind her. He bowed slightly and waved his gnarled free hand toward the vacated seat.

"Ma'am, would you like to sit down?" he said.

Mother Lode

"Barton's General Store" hung over the door in faded red letters. It was a gray, clapboard building in the small town of Wells on the road to Barkerville. Inside, dusty canned goods lined narrow aisles. The corners were cluttered with miscellaneous household items, brooms and pails, scrub brushes and shovels, cans of paint and wash basins. One shelf behind the counter held blue jeans and work shirts. Only in one respect was this store different from most of the other old-fashioned general stores that used to be common throughout Canada (and the United States, for that matter). Up above the shelves along the wall were gold pans (made of stainless steel) and surplus Hudson's Bay blankets to be used for sluice-box matting, items that placed this store firmly in goldmining country.

It was a cloudy August morning when we stopped to buy some soft drinks and chocolate bars. The man behind the counter was about average height, with wisps of white hair over a bronzed, bald head. He was perhaps sixty but well preserved. The air of placid authority in his face led me to believe he must be Mr. 's.

"Good morning."

"Mornin'."

"Rather unseasonable weather?"

"Good gold-pannin' weather. Not too hot to shovel."

"Are you a real goldminer?" my five-year-old exclaimed.

Barton shook his head. "Nope. Too smart for that. My great-great-grandfather came here in 1859 as a merchant. Made more money sellin' food to the miners than most of the miners did diggin' gold. Smart man, my great-great-grandfather. My great-grandfather, grandfather, and father did the same. And me, I'm just carryin' on the family tradition."

"I wouldn't think there would be very many miners for you to sell supplies to these days."

"Not many," he admitted, "but there are tourists headin' for Barkerville, people who come to see the diggin', not to do it—people like yourself." He smiled. "Besides, the miners will be back."

"You mean, the world price of gold going up and the economic uncertainty will bring back the prospectors?"

"The world price of gold don't mean a thing. Prospectin' ain't a business. It's people lookin' for somethin'. It's the gold fever." Barton's eyes lit up. "The gold itself, there's magic in it. People will always come lookin' for it as long as there's people. It's excitement—it's the gold itself."

The gold itself. There was something about the way Barton said it that transformed his whole personality. Perhaps that helped explain why he was here. That was what kept him in a quiet little store, waiting for the gold rush to begin again so he, too, could get rich quick as his great-great-grandfather had done—riches that the succeeding generations had gradually let slip away by continuing to sell here. Boom and bust affected more than just the miners. I could see in him the magic and the attraction of the "gold itself" that he talked about. It *was* fascinating. And I was looking on from the outside, a mere tourist, a spectator from a new age of spectator sports, while he was an actor from a bygone era when everyone had been an actor—everyone in Barkerville anyway. Even Barton's great-great-grandfather, who had come here to sell to the miners, was just as much infected by the gold fever as any of them ever were.

I saw the evidence of that same gold fever the next day in Barkerville itself. On the surface, it is only a hundred or so gray buildings huddled on the bank of a rock-strewn creek bed, some sinking into the brush and earth, a few restored as monuments to the past. But it exudes a romance, a mystery, an attraction that lures tourists as it once lured miners from the far corners of the world. "The largest city west of Chicago and north of San Francisco" in its heyday in the late 1850s and early 1860s, it was home to thousands of miners, with thousands more in the surrounding hills. A transitory city in the midst of a wilderness. A metropolis erected overnight in a vast emptiness that five years earlier had known only a handful of white men. The golden miracle that opened up a virgin territory and laid the foundations for a province now known as British Columbia. The beckoning outpost toward which the silver thread of the Canadian Pacific Railway made its way as to a homing signal and made thinkable the dream of a vast nation in which the Christian God would have dominion from sea to sea. A mirage which sprang up overnight and just as quickly fell back into the oblivion of a ghost town. Its last permanent resident, a lone holdout from a bygone era, died in 1974.

On our visit, there was still a typical miner's cabin, small and dark, made out of logs. A wooden cot in the corner. An iron stove in the center. Newspapers on the wall and a mannequin miner mending worn wool socks forever. Such a stark, lonely life. But he was willing to put up with all this for the prospect of gold. Put up with it? Why, he lived in a log cabin with a dirt floor, ate poorly out of a tin can or a blackened pot, was separated from his family and loved ones, and considered himself the happiest man on earth if only he discovered *gold* on his claim!

All the diversions in Barkerville were just that, diversions from the real heart of the place, window dressing, a facade. The Theatre Royal. The library. The saloons (tiny little places holding no more than a dozen miners each—not at all like the large gambling casinos of cinematic westerns). Even the three or four "sporting houses" (again, simply small log cabins with two or three rooms for the "girls"—eight or nine prostitutes for thousands of miners). All of these colorful institutions hold more attraction for modern tourists than they did for the goldminers of a century ago. Barkerville, the real Barkerville, was not exactly the normal picture we have of a wide-open mining town. There were as many churches as there were sporting houses. Most of the miners probably couldn't have afforded the "girls" even if they had been so inclined. They worked hard all day and got just enough gold to feed themselves—and some of them not even that. Besides, they were no more free of restraints than most people today. A malnourished prostitute in a tiny, cold cabin—not the high life really. All these diversions were little more than desperate attempts to keep life bearable until the miners found gold and struck it rich. They were diversions, not the main attraction. They were distractions from the central quest.

The boot hill cemetery at Barkerville told the same story—of disappointment, denial of the dream the miners came seeking. Reading over the tombstones, one learns that the miners died young and ingloriously—mostly of pneumonia and malnutrition. Almost none were killed in gunfights over claims. Seventeen, eighteen, nineteen, and twenty years old. The ones who survived longer sometimes brought their wives with them to cook decent meals—and the wives died in their places. In childbirth perhaps. Many of the children died as babies and were buried there also. The cemetery was started for a twenty-year-old miner who fell in a nearby mineshaft and broke his back. He is typical somehow of the many who came seeking gold but found only a grave, who came seeking glory and adventure but found only a lonely death far from anyone who cared and loved them.

Yet, one can imagine even the gravediggers intently watching the soil as they threw it up, hoping even in this act of decency to see yellow paydirt and strike it rich. Whatever its other activities and whatever its diversions and claims, Barkerville was a community dedicated to a single purpose. Gold fever burned in every heart. Every man came by choice, not by birth, and by a long, arduous journey to boot—by ship to Victoria, up the Fraser River by steamer, then overland on foot by the Cariboo Trail. They trudged along the precipitous cliffs of the treacherous Fraser River

Canyon, over mountains, and through the dusty heat and dense forests of the Cariboo country. They followed much of the same road that I had travelled, except for my modern detour down through Wells to Barkerville. Even Wells is named not for water, but for a miner. Barton's great-great-grandfather came over the same rough road—to run a mercantile business. Yet, it must have been the love of gold that brought him too.

"So, you think that this area will come back as a goldmining center?" I asked him. "Do you think modern men are still susceptible to gold fever?"

"Shucks, people don't change. They're the same as they always was—ever since some ape picked up a shiny rock on a creek bottom two million years ago and, just like that, he became a man. It's the gold that makes man what he is.

"But is there gold still left to find here? Didn't the miners all leave because the gold petered out?"

"Naw," Barton snorted. "All that mess you see up the creek at Barkerville. All that hoopla and restored goldminin' town nonsense, why, it didn't even scratch the surface, it's barely a drop in a bucket. They only picked up what gold the creek washed down to them out of the mountains. They was too lazy to go up and do real work—hard rock minin' for the mother lode."

Too lazy? The next day I saw a shaft just above Barkerville that some fool had carved by hand, twisting and turning through solid rock in search of gold. I don't think he could have found it. As Barton said, the gold at Barkerville was not in the rock valley walls, but in the stream bed, washed down from the mountains. But the miners didn't just go out and pick up gold nuggets along the creek banks. Too lazy? They would spend all day from dawn to dusk panning or shovelling gravel into sluice boxes under a hot sun—and at the end of the day have only a handful of grains of gold. Maybe once in a while they would find a nugget— but that would soon go to men like Barton's great-great-grandfather for such commodities as eggs—at two dollars a dozen, hauled all the way up from Victoria.

Too lazy? For miles around Barkerville there are no tall trees. In old pictures, there are no trees at all. The virgin forest was all chopped down by hand and turned into cabins and sluice boxes and shovel handles and water barrels and saloons and sporting houses and churches. When the town burned down, it was all rebuilt in three weeks.

Too lazy? A huge pile of slag stands at the entrance to Barkerville. Billy Barker himself, considered by many to be a fool, came down the creek from earlier diggings to Barkerville and dug a shaft down into the river bank for ten feet before he struck the old river bed—and then the gold had to be dug out and drawn up by hand. Billy Barker dug out millions of dollars worth of gold and died a pauper.

The historians say the site of Barkerville is undermined and honeycombed with tunnels and shafts. At the sixty-foot level, there is even a shaft, big enough to stand up in and two miles long, to drain out the water from the mining shafts above. Were these men too lazy?

I suppose in a sense they were. They hoped to work hard for a couple of years so they could quit, so they would not have to spend a lifetime earning their daily bread by the sweat of their brow. They wanted to strike it rich so they could retire in luxury. Some of them did. Most of them didn't. Even many of those who found gold were not quite satisfied and wasted it all in a fruitless search to find an even bigger cache of gold. Gold fever. On average, the pay of the miners for the work they did was appallingly small. But it was uneven. Some got nothing at all, while others got rich. The allure of gold fever is the hope of being one of the lucky ones, like a modern-day lottery winner.

There is another sense in which the miners were lazy. They took gold where they found it. They never attempted the harder task of asking where it came from, of tracing the gold to its source.

"But is there still gold in this area?" I asked Barton again. "Didn't the gold peter out?"

"Oh, the miners picked up a lot of what was layin' about, what the creek has washed down over the last few thousand years. There's not much of that left where the miners looked for it."

"You mean there are other places, if the stream bed moved for instance?"

"Oh yeah, there's that. No one knows which way the old stream bed turned below Barkerville. I know an old prospector, nearly eighty, who thinks he knows where it went—but he's too old, and his sons are not inclined to prospect. They got jobs and families down near Vancouver. Also, that drainin' shaft is probably silted up with some gold by now. Gold's still washin' out of the mountains. And that's the thing! All this is just scratchin' the surface, pickin' up the leavins the creek brings down to you. But the mother lode, the source of the gold, why, it's never been found. It's still hidden up there somewhere in the mountains."

"Didn't anyone ever try to find it?"

"A few have, but they didn't really know what they was doin', and they gave up after a couple of years. To find the mother lode, the source of the gold, takes generations maybe—one man gets closer, and then his son gets closer still until someday one generation finds it. You gotta stick at it—like my great-great-grandfather, my great-grandfather, my grandfather, my father, and me. Them miners, the next generation quits maybe—like old Bill's kids. He thinks he knows where the stream bed gold went, but they won't go and dig it up for him. Them miners is all interested in gettin' rich quick, they're out for themselves, not for furtherin' the whole operation. If they personally can't get rich quick in a couple of years, they're not interested. Why, Barkerville was in decline ten years after it started. Half the miners had died or gone home or somewhere else where the prospects were brighter, and nobody was comin' to take their places. It's all just playin', gold fever—it passes like a fever—you either die of it or get cured. There's no longsufferin', no patience. There's nobody would look for and find the real mother lode, the source of the gold."

I was left with a strange impression of Barton, as a cherub standing at the gates to Barkerville, keeping vigil, waiting for the Chosen One to come with the key to unlock the secret of Barkerville's long-sought treasure. It was the vigil of all the Bartons, generation after generation, waiting, not seeking themselves but faithfully waiting for one who would.

It was strange, I thought, after all the frenzied activity Barkerville had seen. Thousands of them had toiled. Hundreds had died in the attempt. They had dug out piles of gold, enough to build and furnish three or four churches and much else besides. Yet, they had lived mean, squalid, uncomfortable lives in the midst of all that treasure washing down from the hills. And they had never found the source of the gold, the mother lode, because they had not looked for it. As Barton said, in spite of their arduous toil, they were lazy, and I was reminded that sloth was one of the seven deadly sins.

"But does the mother lode exist? Isn't it possible that all the gold washed down from the hills long ago and there is no more left in the mountains to find?"

"Yes, it's possible—and that's why it will never be found by someone who wants to get rich quick, someone interested only in the gold. It has to be found by someone willin' to take that risk that the whole search is a waste of time. To find the source of the gold requires a lifetime commitment."

The Crosswalk

"Paul, would you mind having a talk with Mr. Wood?"

Paul looked up to see the director of Winterhaven Seniors Home standing there. "Sure, Mrs. Winter. What's the problem?"

"Mr. Wood likes to go across the road and sit in the park when the weather is nice, but he never uses the crosswalk in front of our building. He walks a block and a half down the street to the next crosswalk. It is a hard walk for him coming back up the hill."

"Okay," Paul said. "I'll talk to him tomorrow."

*****

The next morning, Paul was waiting when Mr. Wood came out of the building. The old man was stooped over, leaning on his two canes.

"Good morning, Mr. Wood," Paul said. "Could I talk to you for a moment?"

"Good morning, Paul," the old man answered. "What would you like to talk about?"

"Would you like to sit down on the bench here while we talk?" Paul suggested.

"No, thanks," Mr. Wood answered. "Once I sit down, it takes a lot of effort to get back up."

Paul smiled. "The arthritis isn't getting any better?"

Mr. Wood smiled back. "I didn't expect it to."

"Are you heading over to the park this morning?"

"Yes. I spent most of my life working outside. I feel cooped up if I am inside too long."

"Can I ask you a question?" Paul asked.

"Of course."

"Why do you walk all the way to the crosswalk down the hill? Why don't you use the crosswalk right here?"

"What crosswalk?"

"The crosswalk right there," Paul said, pointing.

Mr. Wood looked. "Do you mean those colored rectangles stretching across the street?"

"Yes, that's it."

"That's a crosswalk? Crosswalks are usually white. That's confusing."

"It's a rainbow crosswalk. The rainbow is a symbol for the LGBTQ community."

"I thought the rainbow was a symbol of God's promise that he would never destroy the earth again by flood, no matter how evil people become."

"That's just an old myth. In the modern, world, the rainbow represents LGBTQ people."

"Who are LBG...whatever it was...people?"

"People who are lesbian, gay, bisexual, transsexual, or questioning their sexuality. The different colored rectangles show that all people, no matter how different, are still beautiful."

"The Bible says that same-sex sex is sinful."

"Again, that is an antiquated view from a former time."

"I didn't say it," Mr. Wood said.

"Good for you," Paul replied. "No one has the right to say that another person is wrong or evil. That is a hateful attitude. And that is why rainbow crosswalks are important. They show that all people are good and acceptable and no one has the right to condemn someone else."

"You mean they are intended to teach tolerance?" Mr. Wood asked.

"Oh, much more than tolerance," Paul replied. "They are a way for society as a whole to affirm LGBTQ people. It is not enough to tolerate them or not discriminate against them while still thinking they are abnormal or evil or somehow less worthy than other people. The community must affirm them as LGBTQ."

"You are saying that we must not only accept homosexuals as people but also affirm their sexuality and their sexual activity?"

"Yes, precisely, because that is inherent in who they are."

"That means that when they use rainbow crosswalks, people are not only accepting LBG people as people but also homosexuality itself and everything that goes with it?"

"I suppose you could say it that way."

"Does that work for other groups?"

"That is what it's all about," Paul said. "That is the point of the crosswalks. They say that every color, every person, is good and beautiful."

"So, we should affirm vegetarians as vegetarians and Chinese people as Chinese people?"

"Yes!"

"And Buddhists as Buddhists?"

"Yes."

"And Muslims and Christians too?"

"Yes."

"So, society shows its acceptance and affirmation of LBG people by putting in rainbow crosswalks and walking on them?"

"Yes."

"Then how would we show acceptance of Christians? By wearing a cross or joining a march for Jesus?"

"I would never wear a cross," Paul said. "Christians say I am sinful for being a gay man. Their ideas are hateful."

"Christians' ideas are wrong?"

"Yes, because they refuse to accept other people," Paul explained.

"I thought you said that no one has the right to say another person is wrong or evil?"

"But that can't apply to people who are hateful," Paul argued. "I am not criticizing Christians as people but only some antiquated and obviously wrong ideas. Look. Sometimes people's actions and their ideas are incorrect. But that is not what I'm talking about here. Being gay is not about what I do or what I believe. It is who I am. It is my identity. I was born this way. All people are beautiful and should be accepted for who they are, but that does not mean that we have to accept every outdated idea or condone hateful actions. Do you understand?"

"Yes, I think so," old Mr. Wood said. "In fact, I think I understand very well. You see, I was born a child of God—twice."

"You are no longer a child, Mr. Wood."

"I wouldn't be so sure about that." The older man was quiet for a moment. "Thank you for the talk, Paul. It has been enlightening. Have a good day."

Then Mr. Wood shuffled off, leaning on his canes, heading down the hill.

*****

"Did you talk with Mr. Wood, Paul?" Mrs. Winter asked.

"Yes, but I don't think it did any good. He listened to me, and then he didn't use the rainbow crosswalk but walked down the hill to the other one."

"Oh, dear."

"I think he must have dementia," Paul added. "He doesn't think straight."

The Marriage Commissioner

My first impression was that they were an attractive young couple. Early twenties. Quite normal looking.

"We want to get married," he said as they came up to the counter at city hall. He had neat, brown hair and a pleasant face.

"That's lovely!" I enthused. I have a soft spot for young love.

He didn't smile back as I had expected. He didn't look unhappy, more like he was surprised and a little confused.

"The first step is to get a marriage license," I explained. "Have you got that yet?"

"No," he answered.

"You can get that now. I will need to see two pieces of identification," I said as I opened the right form on the countertop computer.

He produced a driver's license and a birth certificate, and I entered the information onto the form. The cards identified him as Anthony David Tunstall, age twenty-four.

His companion, long black hair framing a finely defined brown face, produced her identification from a brown purse. The cards said she was Annamaria Charina Lauzon, age twenty-three.

I entered her information into the computer, along with their addresses and phone numbers. In answer to my question, he said he was an apprentice carpenter and had never been married before. She said she worked as a bookkeeper and had also never been married.

He paid the fee with cash, and I printed the license and a receipt and handed them to him.

"When are you getting married?" I asked out of friendly curiosity.

The young man seemed confused. "Um, can't we do that here?" he asked.

"Yes, of course," I answered. "Mr. Winfield, one of our staff, is a marriage commissioner. You will have to first make an appointment with him for a consultation, to discuss the particulars of the wedding, and then you can agree on a date when he can perform the wedding."

"Can't we do it now?" the young man asked.

"Well, that might be possible," I said. "Mr. Winfield likely has some time on his schedule today when you can have the consultation."

"No, I meant can't we get married today?" the young man said.

"Well, I don't know," I said. "The wedding isn't usually scheduled for the same day. We would have to check Mr. Winfield's schedule. But don't you need some time to get ready? Aren't you going to want to get changed for the pictures?"

The young man was dressed in a short-sleeved, checked shirt and casual slacks. The young woman was wearing a T-shirt, new blue jeans, and sneakers.

"What pictures?" The young man asked. "Is that part of the process, like a driver's license photo?"

"No," I said. "It's not required, but don't you want to take some pictures to commemorate the occasion?"

"Not particularly," he answered.

I looked at the young woman, who had hardly said a word to this point, but she remained quiet.

"Do you have witnesses coming?" I asked.

"Witnesses?" The young man looked puzzled.

"Yes, family and friends. Don't you want them present for this?"

"Not really," he said. "If we need witnesses, aren't there people here who could do that?"

"Well, yes, that is possible," I answered. "I just thought you might like somebody you know present."

The young man said nothing. The young woman said nothing too, but I had expected that by now.

I asked, "Have you ever been present at a wedding?"

"No, I don't think so," the young man said.

The young woman just shook her head.

"I'll take you to see Mr. Winfield," I said. "He's officiating at a wedding right now upstairs." I thought it would also give them a chance to see what a wedding looked like.

We took the elevator to the second floor. There was a fairly large lobby with bench seats along the walls. Next to it was a large meeting room behind smoked glass, as well as a corridor leading to more meeting rooms and offices. I led the couple toward the glass doors leading to the first meeting room, but did not open them. We looked through the glass.

"Do you see the man in the dark suit at the far end of the room?" I said. "The one facing us? That is Mr. Winfield."

Mr. Winfield is a friendly looking man with thinning, black hair and a neat mustache. I hoped he might put the young couple more at ease.

"Do you see the two men in tuxedos standing in front of Mr. Winfield?" I continued. "Those two men are reciting their vows and getting married."

"To each other?" the young man asked.

"Yes. Mr. Winfield performs heterosexual and homosexual and lesbian marriages. We do not discriminate here. Marriage is open to everyone," I explained. "Do you see all those nicely dressed people in the chairs watching the ceremony? They are the couple's friends and family members, who are here to celebrate this event with them. And do you see the man with the camera over there? He is a professional photographer taking pictures. And the woman in the front row is videotaping the entire ceremony, so the couple will have professional photos and a video to commemorate the day, which the couple can look at whenever they want. The way this couple has done everything can be a model for you, to show you the proper way to get married."

The couple did not seem impressed.

At that point, the elevator door opened. A man in a dark suit and a woman in a long white dress got out, along with half a dozen other well-dressed men and women. They seemed in a party mood.

"That is the next couple getting married," I pointed out in a low voice. "Don't they look happy?!"

The young man and woman beside me didn't disagree. They just looked a little confused or bored.

After a while, the elevator door opened again, and more well-dressed people got out, led by another man in a dark suit and a woman in a long, mauve dress. They immediately went over and greeted the couple who were about to get married.

"The other man in the dark suit is probably the best man," I whispered. "He is likely the groom's best friend or his brother. He is here to support the groom. The woman in the mauve dress is the maid of honor or matron of honor, likely the bride's best friend or a sister. She is here to support the bride. The best man and maid of honor will serve as the official witnesses of the wedding."

By this time, the couple in the meeting room were sitting at a table signing documents.

"They are signing the marriage documents now," I said, indicating the couple. "That makes the wedding official. Mr. Winfield should be out shortly, and you can talk to him then."

The two of them sat down beside me on one of the benches in the lobby, watching what was going on and looking a little bored, waiting.

After a few more minutes, Mr. Winfield came out of the meeting room. I rose to meet him.

"Mr. Winfield," I said, "this is Anthony Tunstall and Annamaria Lauzon. They want to get married."

Mr. Winfield smiled at the couple as they stood up. "Of course. I would be glad to officiate." Turning to me, he asked, "Ms. Sorenson, have you made an appointment for them to come and see me for the consultation, so we can discuss the arrangements?"

I hesitated. "The thing is, Mr. Winfield, they said they want to get married today."

"Today?" he said. "That's somewhat unusual." Turning to the young couple, he added, "We usually recommend a wait of seven to ten days between the consultation and the actual wedding ceremony, but it is not a legal requirement. That much time is usually needed to make all the proper arrangements. I suppose we could do the consultation now. I have a half-hour before that next wedding. But marriage is not something you should rush into. Is there any reason why you need to get married today?"

"Not really," the young man said. "But we're here now. We don't particularly want to have to come back."

"Well," Mr. Winfield said, "I have nothing scheduled after this next wedding. So, you could get married later this afternoon. Are you sure that will be enough time for you to get ready?"

I coughed. "Mr. Winfield, Mr. Tunstall and Ms. Lauzon are not planning on a formal wedding. They said they aren't planning to dress formally or have any pictures taken."

Mr. Winfield frowned. "Oh. Well, perhaps we should go to my office and discuss this further. Ms. Sorenson, will you please come along?"

Mr. Winfield led us down the corridor to his office. He sat down behind his desk, and the couple sat in chairs across from him. I sat on another chair near the door. Mr. Winfield pulled a marriage planning form from his desk drawer.

"Now," he began. "You do not want a very formal wedding, and you aren't planning to have any pictures taken, is that right?"

"Yes," the young man answered.

And do you have friends and family coming?"

"No," the young man said.

Mr. Winfield turned to me. "Ms. Sorenson, have they acquired a marriage license?"

"Yes, Mr. Winfield. We filled out the form, and they paid for the license."

"And there are no impediments?"

"No. They are both of age and say they have never been married before. They were both born in this country."

Mr. Winfield turned back to the couple. "Marriage is a serious step. Are you sure you want to get married? Have you thought about it for a while, or is this something you just decided to do recently?"

"We have known each other for two years," the young man said. "We have talked about it, and we decided a few months ago to get married."

"But you have not invited your friends and family to be here," Mr. Winfield pointed out. "Do your parents support your decision, or are they opposed to you getting married?"

"We told them, and they're fine with it," the young man answered.

"And you, Ms. Lauzon, are your parents in agreement?" Mr. Winfield asked.

The young woman broke her silence. "Yes, they agree with our decision."

"Then why aren't they coming to the wedding? Why don't you want pictures taken?" Mr. Winfield asked.

"Why would they come?" the young man asked. "A few months ago, I bought a new truck. I went to the dealership and signed the agreement to buy the truck, the forms to get the loan, and the insurance papers. My parents knew I was buying the truck, and they thought it was a good idea, but they didn't come to witness me signing the papers or take pictures. I didn't dress up in a suit to buy the truck."

"Acquiring a wife is not the same thing as buying a truck," Mr. Winfield said sternly. "What do you think marriage is anyway?"

The young man paused a moment and then said, "It's a legal document, like a contract. It's an arrangement so we can share health benefits and fill out a joint income tax return, apply for joint loans, that kind of thing."

"Marriage is a legal document, yes," Mr. Winfield said, "but it's more than that. It's a commitment."

"A commitment?" the young man repeated. "That's a contract, a legal agreement, right?"

"Yes, but..." Mr. Winfield seemed to be struggling to find the right words to explain marriage to the young couple. "Well, for one thing, marriage is intended to last longer than a truck."

"The truck loan is for seven years," the young man said. "I've heard that many marriages don't last that long."

"But why do you want to get married?" Mr. Winfield demanded.

"I already explained that," the young man answered. "It makes it easier to share health benefits and apply for joint loans, and there are tax benefits, a lot of financial reasons."

Mr. Winfield turned suddenly to the young woman. "Ms. Lauzon, are you pregnant?" he asked. "Is that why you are getting married? You don't have to get married because you're pregnant nowadays. There are a lot of women who are doing just fine as single mothers. There is no stigma anymore. And if you don't want the baby, well, you could..."

"I am not pregnant," the young lady said evenly.

"Certainly not," echoed the young man.

"What are your plans for after the wedding?" Mr. Winfield said. "Where are you going to live? You are going to live together?"

"Not right away," the young woman said, "but eventually."

"What do you mean by eventually?"

"In a few weeks," the young man answered.

"Then why are you getting married now?" Mr. Winfield persisted. "There must be some reason other than the financial. Why aren't you more excited about it? Are you in love?"

"Why are you asking us these questions?" the young man demanded. "Do you ask other couples these questions? Ms. Sorenson said you don't discriminate. We want to get married. Don't you have to do it, legally, if we ask?"

Mr. Winfield sighed. "Part of my job is to be sure that this is a legitimate marriage. But yes, we do not discriminate." He paused, looking over the wedding planning form. "So, there will be no pictures, no guests. I presume there will be no flowers or other decorations?"

The young man looked hard at the young woman, shrugged, and said, "No."

"Any special music?"

"No."

"Now, have you prepared wedding vows?" Mr. Winfield asked.

The young couple looked confused, as if they didn't understand the question.

"The wedding vows," Mr. Winfield explained. "The commitments you make to each other. Some couples like to write their own vows."

The young man shook his head. "I don't think we want to do that."

"There are formal vows that you can choose from," Mr. Winfield said. "What kind of vows would you prefer—traditional, modern, religious...?"

"Isn't there some kind of standard form you usually use?" the young man asked.

"Standard, it is," Mr. Winfield said. "Will you be exchanging rings?"

"No," the young man said emphatically.

"No rings," Mr. Winfield repeated. "Now, you will still have to pay to rent the meeting room even if there are just the two of you. We have to have the wedding someplace, and that means the room can't be used for other things. The room rental is $450. Then there is my fee of $250 for officiating, the fees to register the marriage, and $50 for each of the witnesses. Are you willing and able to pay these fees?"

"That seems like a lot of money," the young man said. But then he shrugged. "Sure, I can pay that much."

Mr. Winfield looked perplexed. He turned to me. "Ms. Sorenson, will you take this couple back downstairs, complete the rest of the paperwork, and have Mr. Tunstall here pay the necessary fees? And please recruit another employee who could serve as the second witness." He turned to the couple. "I will perform the ceremony when you come back up, after I have finished with the other wedding, in about an hour or so. Will that be all right?"

The young man said, "Sure."

I took the couple back downstairs. They completed the rest of the forms, and the young man paid the fees, using a debit card this time. Then I recruited another member of the staff, Ms. Adams, to serve as the second witness.

When we got back upstairs, the next wedding ceremony was almost finished. This time, I did not bother to explain what was going on. The young couple did not seem interested.

After a few minutes, the doors to the meeting room opened, and the newly married couple, along with their family and friends, poured out into the waiting area. There was a lot of excited talking, laughter, and animated movement, in sharp contrast to the subdued attitude of the young couple sitting beside me on the bench.

About fifteen minutes later, when the crowd had all left, we went into the meeting room. Mr. Winfield indicated that the couple should stand in front of him, and Ms. Adams and I took up our places slightly behind them.

Mr. Winfield began with the introductory remarks: "We are gathered in this place to witness the formal joining of this couple in the legal state of matrimony, according to the order and custom prevailing in our nation. The state of matrimony, as understood by us, is ennobled and enriched by a long and honorable tradition, set in the basis of the law of the land, assuring each participant of equality before the law and of basic human rights. Your marriage must be based on your firm belief in your individual worth and in that of the other, remembering that the pledges you make today will only remain valid as long as you look upon them as an expression of your devotion and freedom. Marriage is therefore not to be entered upon thoughtlessly or irresponsibly but with a proper appreciation of its solemnity and significance and with a due and serious understanding of the ends for which it is contracted."

Mr. Winfield has a deep and solemn voice he uses when he is performing a wedding ceremony, and I love the archaic language. It reminds me of the traditions associated with marriage.

Mr. Winfield continued, "In light of the seriousness of this undertaking, I must ask if there is anyone present who can show just cause why these two persons may not be lawfully joined together in matrimony. Such persons should now declare those reasons or hereafter remain silent."

Mr. Winfield looked around the room. Since there were only the five of us present, he did not pause for long.

Mr. Winfield then asked them each to affirm that there were no legal impediments to their union, which they did, simply repeating the words after him.

Then, Mr. Winfield prepared to have them repeat the standard vows. "Please join your right hands and respond…"

"Do we have to?" the young woman asked, interrupting him.

"What?" Mr. Winfield said. "I'm sorry. Do you have to what?"

"Do we have to hold hands?" she said. "Is that a legal requirement? Is it part of the ceremony?"

"Well," Mr. Winfield said. "It's in the instructions the government gives me, but I suppose technically it is not necessary."

"Okay," she said.

"Okay," Mr. Winfield said. "You don't have to hold hands." Turning to the young man, he continued, "Anthony, do you take Annamaria to be your lawfully wedded spouse? Do you promise to respect the dignity of their person, their inalienable personal rights, their inherent equality, and their right to counsel and consultation in all matters pertaining to your life together? If so, answer, 'I do.'"

The young man answered, "I do."

Then Mr. Winfield asked the young woman the same question, and she answered, "I do."

"Are you going to be exchanging wedding rings?" Mr. Winfield asked.

The young man shook his head. "We already said no."

"Right. Okay, we will skip that part." Mr. Winfield paused. "And now, inasmuch as you have consented to join in legal wedlock before these witnesses, by the governmental authority invested in me, I now pronounce you as duly married. You may now seal these vows with a kiss."

"Kiss?" The young man asked. "Is that legally necessary for us to get married?"

Mr. Winfield took a deep breath. "No, it is not legally necessary." He looked around the empty meeting room. "Look," he said. "You should have more respect for the institution of marriage. Marriage is a serious matter, with long-term implications. The prescribed elements in the wedding ceremony are not there by accident. They represent centuries of tradition and social custom. The declaration that you may now kiss is symbolic of the understanding, going back centuries, that the couple getting married would refrain from physical contact until after they were married. The declaration that you may kiss symbolizes the granting of permission by the state and by society for the couple to now engage in physical contact, in sexual relations. Like everything else in the traditional marriage ceremony, it has deep significance and meaning."

The young man was silent for a few moments. "Are you saying," he asked at last, "that the other couples you married today haven't had sex with each other before they got married?"

"Well, I suppose..." Mr. Winfield started. "Well, really, I have no way of knowing. I suppose nowadays many of them have already been living together for some time. But that does not change the significance of the tradition."

"But that means your tradition doesn't really mean anything," the young man said.

"That's where you're wrong," Mr. Winfield said. "Traditions are very important. They are the glue that holds society together. They are full of meaning. They go on from generation to generation, and each generation invests them with the meanings they choose to pour into them."

The young man seemed to be thinking about that, but he did not respond. After a time, he finally spoke but changed the subject. "Is that it?" he asked. "Are we married now?"

Mr. Winfield sighed. "Yes, you are now married. You just need to go over to that table and sign the documents."

When the documents had been signed, the young couple stood up. "Thank you," the young man said. Then, they turned and walked out the door toward the elevators. They were not holding hands or touching in any way.

Mr. Winfield, Ms Adams, and I just stood there watching them until they had disappeared into the elevator.

"There is something not quite right about that wedding," Mr. Winfield said, breaking the silence. "I think it might be a marriage of convenience, maybe to allow Ms. Lauzon to remain in the country."

"But, according to her birth certificate, she was born here. She's already a citizen," I said. "But I agree that there is something odd about them."

"Then, there must be something else," Mr. Winfield said. "It is certainly not a conventional marriage. They don't appear to be in love. They aren't planning on living together right away. I am not even sure she wants to get married, or maybe he is pressuring her into it."

"Then, why did you agree to marry them?" I asked.

"Because I had no choice. We do not discriminate. I have to marry anyone who can legally do so, who pays the necessary fees, and who asks. I couldn't find a legal reason to refuse them." He sighed. "Maybe it's just young people today. They have no understanding of tradition and the importance and solemnity of marriage. It was as if they were just following some bureaucratic process. Marriage should be much more than that."

I wholeheartedly agreed with Mr. Winfield. As I said, I have a soft spot for young love.

*****

About four weeks later, Mr. Winfield called me on my desk phone and asked me to come up to his office.

I found him staring at his computer.

"Thank you for coming, Ms. Sorenson," he said. "Do you recall that we retain lists of wedding photographers and florists and limousine services for the people who come here to get married? We don't make recommendations or promise to vet these service suppliers. We just add them to the list if they make a request."

"Of course, Mr. Winfield," I answered. "Those lists seem more important than ever with more and more people now coming to city hall to get married."

"Precisely," Mr. Winfield said. "And while we don't promise to vet the people who request to get on the lists, I do at least perform some checks, validate their phone numbers, and look at their websites, for instance."

"Yes, Mr. Winfield. That is very thorough of you. I know you take your job as marriage commissioner very seriously."

"Well, we recently had a request from another wedding photographer to be added to the list. So, I looked at his website. He has apparently been photographing weddings for some time already. He has a lot of sample pictures on his website. Guess what I found when I started scrolling through them?"

Mr. Winfield turned his computer monitor so I could see. The photos were arranged in groups under headings: John and Amy...Pierre and Marguerite...Jordan and Ashley...Tony and Annamaria.

I gasped. "That's that young couple you married a few weeks ago, the couple who said they didn't want any photos taken."

"Yes, Anthony Tunstall and Annamaria Lauzon. They said they didn't want any photos or special clothes or

145

friends and family present. But look at those photos. Look at that dress."

"There's other people in dresses and suits," I said. "And there's a close-up of their wedding rings. When were these photos taken?"

"The date on the photos suggests the weekend before last, about three weeks after I married them."

"Maybe they changed their minds about having a big wedding. Maybe their families talked them into it," I suggested.

"But how could they arrange all this in only three weeks?"

"I don't know," I answered. "Where were the photos taken?"

"See this photo here," Mr. Winfield said. "See the sign in the background? It says Greenway Community Church."

"What are you going to do, Mr. Winfield?"

"I have already started. I looked up the information they gave for the wedding license, and I phoned Mr. Tunstall. Apparently, he has an apartment. I phoned several times, but there was no answer. Then, I phoned the number she gave. A woman answered. She had quite a pronounced accent. I asked for Annamaria, and she said she didn't live there anymore. I asked for a forwarding address, and she gave me Mr. Tunstall's contact information."

"So, what now?"

"I am going to go and check out this Greenway Community Church," Mr. Winfield said. "And I want you to come with me as a witness. There is something seriously wrong here."

*****

We took Mr. Winfield's car and rode in silence most of the way. The building we were looking for was in a residential neighborhood on the west side of the city.

Greenway Community Church was a long A-frame building set at right angles to the street. To the left was a

146

parking lot with a single battered SUV parked in it next to the building. Decades-old oak trees lined the grassy margin around the parking area.

Mr. Winfield parked a few spaces away from the SUV. We got out and walked up a curved, sloped, paved walkway that led to the front door in one end of the A-frame. Doors, actually—four big, green, wooden doors. Mr. Winfield tried each of the doors in turn, but they were all locked.

"There's a doorbell," I said, pointing to a spot beside the last door.

Mr. Winfield pressed it, a distant buzzer could be heard, and nothing happened—for almost a minute. Suddenly, one of the doors swung open. There was an average-looking man of middle age and average height and weight. I recognized him from one of the photos, only this time he wasn't wearing a formal suit but a sports shirt and slacks.

"Hello," he said cheerily. "I'm Pastor Wade Davis. I'm sorry about the locked door, but we have had some problems with vandals. How can I help you?"

"I am Tom Winfield. I am a marriage commissioner at city hall," Mr. Winfield said, "and this is Ms. Sorenson."

"Come in," the man said. "We can talk in my office."

I exchanged glances with Mr. Winfield. Was it safe to go into a locked building with this man?

But we went in. The man led us along a carpeted lobby area to a glass-walled office at the end. We walked into it through an open door and then across it and through another door into a second office. This one was larger, with solid walls, but he left the door open. There was a large wooden desk with bookshelves lining the walls behind it, but the man led us over to a cluster of plush chairs grouped around a round coffee table.

"Can I get you some coffee or tea?" the man asked.

"No, thank you," Mr. Winfield replied.

"So, what can I do for you?" the man asked.

"As I told you, I am the marriage commissioner at city hall," Mr. Winfield said, "and I saw these photos on a wedding photographer's website." He pulled the photos out of his briefcase and spread them out on the coffee table.

The man leaned over and looked at the photos. "Ah, yes. Tony and Annamaria," he said.

"The thing is," Mr. Winfield went on," I married Mr. Tunstall and Ms. Lauzon at city hall three weeks before these photos were taken."

"So, you're wondering why they got married twice?" the man said. He raised his eyebrows and sat back in his chair. "They didn't really. The state has defined marriage as a legal contract dealing largely with financial issues and legal obligations. That legal contract was what Tony and Annamaria signed at city hall." He paused and smiled. "I am not a lawyer or an accountant. I don't write contracts. No government documents were produced here at the church. We did not duplicate what was done at city hall."

Mr. Winfield looked skeptical.

"I am not a government agent," the man continued. "As a government agent, I would have to do exactly what the government says. The government would tell me who to marry and how to marry them. It would prescribe the vows to be used and everything else. The government's desire to control things is perfectly demonstrated by the fact that you are here asking me questions."

Mr. Winfield was not intimidated by this speech. "If that is so," he asked, "how do you explain these photos?"

"That was a religious ceremony," the man answered. "Tony and Annamaria were here in the presence of God and in the presence of their friends, their family, and their church community. Tony and Annamaria covenanted together to love and honor each other and to care for each other when they are sick or in trouble or in need of anything. They agreed to put the other person's needs first, ahead of their own. They promised to be faithful to each other for their entire lives, no matter what happens. And they promised to raise their children to love and obey God, to nurture them in the Christian faith. And they asked God to bless their efforts and enable them to keep their promises.

That was a purely religious occasion, much different from the legal contract they signed at city hall."

"I don't believe it," Mr. Winfield said. "You said they promised to love each other. But they didn't show much love or excitement when they were at city hall. They refused to kiss or hold hands, and they didn't want any friends or family present."

"They were signing a government document, a contract," the man said. "What did you expect? You don't have a big ceremony or invite a lot of people to watch you fill out government paperwork."

"One other thing," Mr. Winfield said. "Where are Mr. Tunstall and Ms. Lauzon now? Why are you hiding them?"

"I am not hiding them," the man said. "They are on what I believe you would call their honeymoon. They're expected back by the end of the week."

*****

When we were back in the car, Mr. Winfield didn't start it. He just sat there staring ahead. I could tell he was thinking hard.

"Well," he said at last. "I don't think there's anything we can do. He doesn't seem to have broken any laws." He paused. "But people like that are dangerous. They don't conform to the social norms that govern the lives of the rest of us. Their primary loyalty is not to our country, our government, or our social values. They can't be trusted. They are misfits, bigots, and revolutionaries."

Mr. Winfield is a wise and discerning man, deeply dedicated to his role as marriage commissioner.

The Play's the Thing

"I got the part!" Joan enthused as she burst through the door.

"Huh?" George said. "Part of what?"

"Trixie Dixon."

"Who's that?"

"I am."

George was getting annoyed. "What are you talking about?"

"I got the part of Trixie Dixon in the play."

"What play?"

"The play the Happy Valley Players are putting on."

"Who are they? I thought you were getting involved with the local theater group here in Mud Valley."

"I am," Joan explained, "but Wolf thought Mud Valley Dramatic Society didn't sound elegant enough, so he changed the name."

"Wolf? There's talking animals in the play? Like in Little Red Riding Hood?"

"No. Wolf Fritzenberg. He's the new director of the society. He trained at a dramatic arts school in New York, and he's a genius."

"What kind of a name is Wolf?"

"I think it's short for Wolfgang. He's bringing in a lot of new ideas. He's such a professional and a very charming and sophisticated man. He's changing things. They're going to be so much better."

"What's this about you getting a part?" Joan's husband asked. "I thought you were only going to be involved as a helper with costumes and stuff."

"I was, George, but Wolf saw me backstage, and he immediately said I had something special. He said I was wasted backstage. He wants me to play Trixie Dixon—that's the lead role next to his. He says I could have a future in professional theater. This is so exciting!"

George was speechless.

"Aren't you excited for me?" Joan asked.

"It's a lot..."

"Yes, it's a big opportunity. And Wolf is such a visionary. He has such a professional understanding of the theater. Such wisdom! He's always saying such wise things! For instance, he says, 'If you can do it in real life, you can do it onstage.'"

*****

For the next several weeks, George got used to eating warmed-up leftovers and cold, thrown-together meals and doing extra chores around the house. And hearing glowing accounts of how wonderful and wise and insightful and exciting and charming Wolf was. It was "Wolf this" and "Wolf that," which George found even more nauseating than the food he was reduced to eating.

"You should really come to see me practice," Joan said repeatedly. "I'm sure you would feel better about this if you could just see what I'm doing."

George kept putting her off, but one day, on his way home from work, he stopped in when rehearsal was almost over for the day. He walked through the door into the darkened theater and stood still in the shadows, watching. Onstage, Joan was standing talking face to face with a slim man of medium height. He had chiseled features and black, curly hair down to his shoulders.

"I love you so much, Clive," Joan said earnestly. "But I'm afraid of Bruno. He's so cruel and violent. I don't know what he would do if he found out about us."

"He's a brute, unworthy of a woman of your beauty and grace," the man said as he reached out to caress Joan's cheek.

"You don't know my husband. You don't know what he is capable of," Joan said.

"Then we'll just have to find a way to get you away from him and keep him from ever finding you," the man said. "Trust me, Trixie. We'll find a way."

"Oh, Clive," Joan breathed.

They embraced in a long, passionate kiss. When they parted, Joan was breathing heavily and seemed entranced.

"And the curtain closes here," the man named Clive said. (George supposed his real name was Wolf.) "And then it reopens for the closing scene." He turned toward a woman standing at the edge of the stage. "Where's my Bruno?"

The woman stepped forward. She was dressed in a baggy sweater and a calf-length, dark skirt and was carrying a clipboard. George recognized her as Mildred Peabody, the local librarian.

"I'm sorry, Mr. Fritzenberg," she said timidly. "He just texted me. He had an accident and broke his leg. He isn't coming."

"Amateurs!" Wolf said. "When they're told to break a leg, they take it literally. Where's the understudy?"

"We...we don't have an understudy," Mildred said timidly. "It's such a small part..."

"Then who's he?" Wolf demanded, pointing to the back of the theater.

"George?" Joan said hesitantly. "Hi..."

"Come here," Wolf demanded.

George slowly walked down the aisle.

"He's perfect!" Wolf said. "Mildred, get him prepped."

"But he hasn't practiced, and the opening is in two days," she said with a shocked look on her face.

"He's got one stupid line!" Wolf shouted. "Surely, he can learn that in two days!"

Joan moved to the front of the stage. "George, thank you so much for coming," she said. "Would you mind?"

George shrugged.

Mildred beckoned George to some steps at the edge of the stage. He walked up the steps and followed Mildred behind the curtain. She led him over to a table, picked up a replica gun, and handed it to him.

Mildred said, "Hold the gun down at your side so the audience won't be able to see it. When I tell you, go through that door onto the stage. Stand there inside the door. Joan will say a line, and then you say to Mr. Fritzenberg, 'I won't let you steal my woman.' Have you got that?"

"I won't let you steal my woman," George said.

"Try to say it with more feeling next time," Mildred said.

"Okay," George said.

"Then, Mr. Fritzenberg will say a line. Don't be in a rush. Make sure the other actors are finished speaking their lines. It's okay if there is a pause. It helps build suspense. Then, raise the gun, point it at Mr. Fritzenberg, and pull the trigger. There will be a bang."

George waited a moment. "Then what?"

"Oh," Mildred said. "Two men will grab your arms. It's okay if you struggle a little, but not too much. After that, you don't have to do anything. They will lead you offstage."

George nodded.

Mildred picked up a stick and rattled it across the top of a table.

George could hear Joan speaking onstage in a startled voice: "What was that?"

"What was what? I didn't hear anything," Wolf replied.

"No, I heard something," Joan insisted. "What if Bruno came home early?"

Mildred touched George on the arm. "Go in," she said quietly.

George opened the door and walked through. Joan and Wolf were lying on a bed. They sat up suddenly.

"Bruno," Joan said, her voice shaking with fear. "Don't be angry."

There was a pause, and then George said, "I won't let you steal my woman."

Wolf raised his head and said defiantly, "She's not your woman anymore. You don't deserve her. She's free of you now."

George stared, then slowly raised the gun and pulled the trigger. Wolf flopped violently back down onto the bed.

"You brute!" Joan shouted. "You've killed him, Bruno!"

She threw herself onto Wolf's prostrate body, sobbing inconsolably.

Behind George, the door burst open, and two men charged in. Turning his head, George recognized the Proctor brothers, big men who worked in the local mill. They seized George's arms, and one of them pulled the gun from his hand.

"You're under arrest," Rick, the one on his left, said.

George, surprised, struggled a bit, but the two men were much stronger than he was. They quickly dragged him out through the door.

Backstage, George stood there, confused. He could hear dialogue leaking through the door from the stage.

"Are they gone?" Clive asked.

"Yes. It's safe," Trixie responded enthusiastically. "Your plan worked perfectly! I saw Bruno loading his gun last night, and after he went to sleep, I exchanged the bullets for the blanks you gave me."

There was more dialogue between Clive and Trixie, but George did not hear it. His mind was elsewhere.

*****

"Thank you so much for coming, George, and for even agreeing to fill in as Bruno," Joan said that night. "It means so much to me. What did you think of my performance?"

"Oh, you were very good," George said. "You were very believable. I had no idea you could appear to be one person at home and be a very different person onstage."

"That's all Wolf's doing," Joan said. "He is such a good teacher."

"I can believe it," George said. "But I didn't really like that long kiss you gave him."

"Wolf says that it is important that everything looks and feels authentic onstage. Wolf says that if something can happen in real life, then it can also happen onstage. So, it has to be authentic. But the difference is that it doesn't mean anything. It's just acting."

George was silent.

"Tomorrow night is the dress rehearsal," Joan said. "Are you ready for that?"

"What's a dress rehearsal?"

"That's the final practice, when we run through the play from beginning to end in full costume."

"Costume? What am I supposed to wear?" George asked.

"Exactly what you wore today. In fact, Wolf told me to be sure not to wash it. Your clothes need to look authentic, like you just came home from work."

George thought for a moment. "In that final scene, where you and Wolf are in bed together, what are you wearing?"

Joan hesitated. "Well, not much. But again, it has to look and feel authentic, to convince the audience that it is real even if it isn't. Wolf says that if something can happen in real life, then it can also happen onstage. But he also says that being onstage is like being in an alternative world, a parallel universe. What happens onstage has to be real, but it has no effect in the real world."

"Sort of like what happens in Vegas stays in Vegas?"

"Exactly."

*****

The next night, George sat silently in a corner backstage, listening to the relationship of Clive and Trixie developing onstage, on the other side of the wall. He could imagine the long kiss at the end of the second last scene.

Mildred Peabody came to him. "Are you ready?" she asked.

George nodded.

She handed him the pistol, which he stuffed into his pants pocket. Then, she took the wooden stick and rattled it across the prop table.

"What was that?" Trixie said onstage.

"What was what? I didn't hear anything," Clive answered.

"No, I heard something. What if Bruno came home early?" Trixie pleaded.

George burst through the door. Clive and Trixie were lying on the bed, naked arms and upper torsos emerging above the covers.

Trixie sat up suddenly. "Bruno," she said, her voice shaking with fear. "Don't be angry."

There was a pause, and then Bruno growled, more forcefully than the last time. "I won't let you steal my woman."

"She's not your woman anymore," Wolf said. "You don't deserve her. She's free of you now."

Bruno stared, then slowly pulled the gun from his jacket pocket, raised it up, and pulled the trigger. There was a loud report, and Clive flopped violently back onto the bed.

"You brute!" Trixie shouted. "You've killed him, Bruno!" Leaning down onto Clive's blood-soaked body, Joan was still for a moment. Then she repeated, "You brute! You've killed him!" She paused. "George! You've killed him! Why? Why?"

The Preston brothers burst through the door and seized George's arms, taking the gun from his hand.

George did not resist. "Why?" he said. "Because if it can be done in real life, it can be done onstage. And what is done onstage stays onstage. It is just acting, an alternative universe. It has no effect on real life."

Thou Shalt Not

The words troubled him. John read them over again. They seemed so archaic. So judgmental. So negative. So out of keeping with the rest of the book. He read them again: "Thou shalt not."

The next day, he returned to them again. Every time he read them, he felt the same things. Dirty. Sad. Confused.

So, he returned to them the day after that. The words continued to trouble him.

For a while, he tried to ignore them, pretend they weren't there. He didn't read them again for several days. But they remained there in the back of his mind, niggling away at his peace.

And so it went for a long time. For weeks. Months. Years.

In the back of his mind, an idea began to form, like a hidden callous gradually formed by the constant niggling. He wasn't even aware of it at first. After a while, when he first became aware of it, he dismissed it outright. Then, in time, he paused a few seconds before dismissing it. After even more time, he began to entertain it for a bit. Question it. Examine it. Think about it. Ponder it. Finally, he put it into words.

What if he removed those words from the book? It was unthinkable. But then he began to think it. It would still be a good book. A well-loved book. Perhaps even a better book.

This went on for a long time. And then, almost without thinking, he did it. In a sudden surge of emotion, when his mind was distracted and thinking about something else, on a day when the sun was shining, the flowers were blooming, and the birds were singing, he opened the book, tore out the page, and dropped it into the recycling bin.

Nothing happened. The sun went on shining. The flowers went on blooming. The birds went on singing. And he loved the book more than ever. It was his joy, his inspiration. It was even better without those offending words.

And then one day, while reading his beloved book, he came across some other words that troubled him. He had not noticed them before. But they troubled him just as the other words had.

The process went more quickly and was easier this time. It required less thinking. Less pondering. Less soul searching. There were fewer doubts.

In only a few weeks, he reached a decision. He opened the book and tore out that page too. The book was even better now, he reflected. More inspirational. More comforting. Less troubling. The sun went on shining. The flowers went on blooming. The birds went on singing. And he was happy. Content.

One day, another thought struck him. Maybe he should examine the book closely and see if there were any other troubling words. And so, he read it through, carefully. At first, he marked any troubling words he found. Later, he went back and examined them again. He thought about them deeply. Some he decided could be kept. They were not all that troubling. But some just didn't seem to fit into his beloved book. They didn't belong. And so, he removed them, methodically and thoughtfully. He cut them out carefully, leaving no ragged edges to show where they had been removed.

There were only a few pages that he had removed. The book was now perfect, seamless. He loved it even more. He read it over and over again. And the more he read, the more he was convinced that he had been right to remove the troubling words, the bothersome pages.

His life went on as it had before. The sun went on shining. The flowers went on blooming. The birds went on singing. And he was happy. Content.

But no life is without its ups and downs. One day, John woke up feeling sad. He wasn't sure why. The feeling persisted. He looked at the shining sun, the blooming flowers, and the flitting and soaring birds, but they brought no solace on this day.

He turned to his book, his beloved book. There were words there that always brought him comfort and joy, one set of words in particular. He flipped through the book to where he thought the words should be, but they weren't there. He skimmed all the pages in that section of the book, but the comforting words weren't there. He read through that whole section of the book carefully, word for word, but he couldn't find the comfort he sought.

That night, he sat down and began reading the book from the beginning. The entirety of his beloved book. It took several evenings of careful study. On the last evening, he closed the book. He was puzzled. Confused. Unhappy. What had happened to his beloved book? Where were the words that had comforted and inspired him, that had always brought him such joy?

Very slowly, the truth came to him. Perhaps those comforting words had been on the back side of one of those pages he had removed, on the back side of one of those pages with the troubling words. With a sigh, he put the book down. The book, his beloved book, no longer brought him joy and comfort. He looked up to face a bleaker future. The sun, hidden by a cloud, was no longer shining. The flowers had withered and died. The birds had ceased their singing.

When the Fire Has Gone Out

The fire was not very spectacular. It was not an overly large building. But, since it was on a hill overlooking the town, it glowed like a beacon in the night.

When the fire had died out, it marked the end of an era. It will not be missed. The destruction of the building was typical of the group that owned it. I had hoped that the building could finally be used for something constructive. It would have been ideal for a bingo hall or a casino or a nightclub, which would have been a real benefit to the town. But the group burned down their own building rather than see it used for anything else, which shows what a destructive force they really were. They are gone now. They left in the night, and I am glad.

I don't know how long they had been here. They were here when I arrived in town ten years ago. I realized right away that they were a serious threat, and I made it my goal to rid the town of them. They were the primary reason I decided to run for mayor, and even after I was elected, it took another seven years to push them out. There should be no room in our town for hate and bigotry.

There were not many of them, maybe only two or three hundred, including the children. That is not a lot in a town of eight thousand. But it is surprising how big an impact that small number could have. Probably, the best way to describe them is to say they were a religious cult of some kind. I never did find out what their specific beliefs were. Their ideas were strange and irrational, out of synch with the rest of the town. They were always against everything. Now they are gone, the roadblocks are gone, and we can get on with building a healthy society.

There were a lot of things in town that they were unhappy about. They didn't like the new curriculum in the school. They were opposed to the proposal to use tax dollars to build the new casino. They were opposed to our plan to extend liquor hours. They didn't like our new adult entertainment district. They didn't seem to understand that these steps were necessary to attract new people and new business to town. I don't know why they were opposed to modernizing the liquor laws, for instance, since any problems associated with drinking were taken care of by the town's AA program. They hated everybody who didn't conform to their narrow and bigoted ideas. They never actually engaged in violence as far as I know, but the threat was there.

The thing that finally convinced them to leave was the Inclusive Community Covenant. It was something that we had worked on for over a year. All civic employees were required to sign the covenant. The covenant stipulated that they would support city policies and promote the city's inclusivity and non-discrimination principles. It also required them to avoid all use of hate speech, which included "moral judgement" language. Members of the parent advisory committee in the school, the downtown business association, sports teams, and other community groups were also required to sign the covenant. As well, the city passed a bylaw saying that the city and its employees would do business only with stores and companies that supported the Inclusive Community Covenant.

It was a master stroke. It was the thing that finally pushed the cult members out of town. But that is not to say that the end did not come without some mystery. After the fire was discovered, it took a lot longer than expected to put it out. This was partly because a number of volunteer firefighters had not showed up to fight the fire. We didn't realize at first where they had gone. Apparently, some cult members had infiltrated the fire department.

That was how we first discovered that the cult members had all left town. In fact, it soon became clear that there were now a significant number of vacant houses. We eventually learned that they had contracted with a large moving company to simultaneously move them out the evening before. The moving company was from out of town and refused to say where the cult members had moved to. We didn't really care as long as they were gone. The bank manager said they had cleaned out or transferred their bank accounts in the preceding few days. All of the houses were listed for sale with an out-of-town realty company, but only a few of them actually sold. We quickly imposed a stringent vacant house tax with large penalties for non-payment. The city took over many of the houses for unpaid taxes before many of the previous owners found out about the tax. We are hopeful that when more people move into town and the vacancy rate is lower, we will be able to sell at least some of them to new people. The depressed property values have cut into city revenues.

We also soon learned just how pervasive the cult's influence had been. Unknown to us, the members of the cult had infiltrated many of the organizations and professions in town. The food bank, the AA program, the seniors' center, the meals on wheels program, daycare centers, and minor league sports and recreation programs all suddenly found themselves short of volunteer workers. Even some of the paid staff were gone. Three school teachers and a road worker with twenty years' experience left. The dentist who offered the free clinic downtown on Saturdays also left. We didn't even know he had been part of the cult. Two of the town's five doctors also moved away. That was a big loss. It is always difficult attracting a doctor to a small town. They seem to prefer the cities, where there is more money.

Some reports, rumors really, have begun circulating in town. First, there were reports of lights having been seen at night up on the hillside in the vicinity of the burned-out building. Then there were stories that some people had begun meeting there in secret. The upper floors had been burned away completely, with just a tangle of charred rubble left, but the building had a concrete basement with a solid concrete roof that had formed the floor of the ground level of the building. Apparently, that had survived the fire. The rumors suggest that some people had cleaned out a space in the basement and were meeting underground. At first, it was thought that they were just kids who had dared each other to go into that dark place or teenagers who were looking for a new place to hang out and party. More recently, some more disturbing rumors have surfaced saying that some people are trying to reform the group that met in that building up on the hill. The rumors suggest they are people who had some loose connection to the group that formerly met there. They included a couple of men who had been in the AA program, some teenagers who had occasionally attended a youth meeting there—the group had apparently been trying to recruit troubled and vulnerable young people to their cult—and a single mother who used to go there to get food handouts. The rumors say the leader might be an older man who was part of the original group but who didn't move away when the others did.

I don't know whether the rumors are true. The local police have their hands full these days, with the recent crime wave and the increased number of violent incidents. But when things calm down a little, I am going to send the police up to the hill to check it out. Our town is a lot better off without that band of troublemakers, and we certainly don't want them to come back.

Dead Man

Preface

"You're a dead man!" Yablonski growled into the phone. Bradley hung up the phone in fear and fled.

Chapter 1

Brian Perry laid down his fork. "Thank you so much. I can't remember the last time I had a home-cooked meal like this."

It was evening and the rays of the late summer sun were still streaming into the dining room of John and Ruby Smyth's modest, century-old home in inner city Winnipeg.

Ruby assessed their guest. He was a slim man of medium height and early middle age. His brown hair was cut short, and his mustache was neatly trimmed. He wore a black, short-sleeved, three-button T-shirt and gray pants.

"Don't you cook for yourself?" she asked.

"Yes, but simple things. Nothing like this." He turned to Ruby's husband, John. "You are a lucky man."

John nodded. "Yes, I am blessed."

"Do you have any family here in Winnipeg?" Ruby asked.

"No," Brian said.

"But you have family back home, maybe even some cousins somewhere?" Ruby persisted.

"No, no family at all. They're all gone."

"I'm so sorry," Ruby said.

"Have you made many friends since coming to Winnipeg?" John asked.

"No, no friends either," Brian said. "And I'm not in touch with any former friends either. I am alone."

"It is not good for a man to be alone," John quoted.

"I suppose you are never alone?" Brian asked.

Ruby looked down the long dining table littered with dishes and silverware. From upstairs came echoes of music, voices, footsteps, and other sounds. "We have four children, Brian. We are never alone. We couldn't be alone if we wanted to."

They laughed.

"Never alone," John repeated softly. "What brought you to Winnipeg?"

"The job. I saw the ad from Best Press looking for an experienced pressman. It was time to make a change, and so I applied."

"Where were you before that?" John asked.

"Um…I was working at another print shop in Calgary."

"Which one?" John asked. "I know some of the people there."

"Fast Eddy's."

"I know that one," John said. "Did you know Harry Dixon there?"

Brian frowned. "Harry Dixon? I think I remember the name, but he was in a different department."

"You know, John," Ruby said. "You should invite Brian to men's group. He could make friends there."

"Men's group?" Brian questioned.

"Sure. It's a group of men who get together every two or three weeks or so, usually on a Saturday or a Friday night, for fun. Sometimes it's just a barbecue, but we've done hikes. We tried paintball one time and quad riding."

*****

"Did you get the sense that Brian wasn't telling us everything?" John asked Ruby later that evening.

165

Ruby thought about that. "Yes. It's odd that he doesn't have any family members or friends anywhere. Of course, we didn't tell him everything either."

"You mean I didn't say that the men's group is associated with our church? Brian needs friends, and I didn't want to scare him off."

"What do you think it would be like to be completely alone like that?" Ruby asked. "What would you do in that situation?"

"I don't know," John said. "I don't think I would feel completely alone. I believe in God, and I would know that He was with me. And that would open up so many more possibilities."

"God places the lonely in families."

"Right," John said. "And he placed us in a big one."

Ruby laughed. "But I think we had something to do with that too."

John smiled and then frowned. "It does seem odd that Brian would come here for that job. It's not that great a job."

"Why did you choose him to invite to dinner?"

"I am not sure that it was a conscious choice or my choice at all really. I went to the press to pick up copies of *Grace* magazine, and he was just standing there in the corner, all alone, watching the press run. When I picked up the copies as they came off the press, he came over, and I explained who I was. He just looked lost. Vic had mentioned that he had a new pressman, so I invited him to dinner on the spur of the moment. I said I like to get to know people I work with."

"You do."

"Yes. I'm not sure who was more surprised when he said yes, him or me."

*****

Panting, Brian plopped down beside John Smyth on the floor in the corner of the gym. "You're not playing much," Brian said. "Don't you like basketball?"

"I enjoy sports and the competition and being with the guys, but for some reason I was never very good at basketball."

Brian looked at John. John was a short, bald, bearded man. Especially short, only five feet tall. "I don't know, John. You look like a natural. You should be a great basketball player."

"Yes. Hard to figure, isn't it? But I excel at limbo. Don't even have to bend."

Both laughed.

The smile faded from Brian's face. "This is the third time I have been to one of these men's events. You never mentioned that it was connected to a church."

"You never asked. What difference does it make?"

"That's the thing. There is a difference. These men...I was going to say that they seem at peace. But that's not it. It's not like everything is perfect for them. They have lots of problems. I know because they've talked about them. Which is also weird. They talk about problems that other people would never admit to anyone."

"It's like they have an underlying peace underneath the problems?" John suggested.

"Exactly. Why?"

"Well, remember when you were a kid? No matter what bad things happened to you at school, you knew that your parents loved you and that they would make everything right once you got home."

"That...um...my childhood wasn't quite like that."

"Childhood wasn't like that for some of them too," John said. "But they believe they have a Heavenly Father who loves them like that now."

"A Heavenly Father? You mean God?" Brian questioned.

"Yes."

"That's it? How does that work?"

"Come to church with us this Sunday. Maybe it will help you understand."

"I'll think about it," Brian said. "My turn!" He jumped up and returned to the game.

*****

"It's great to see you at church," John said.

They were standing in the crowded foyer of Central Grace Evangelical Church. It was the end of October, but in Winnipeg that meant that there was already snow on the ground outside.

"Dan Miller said that he would take me ice fishing this winter if I came to church with him," Brian said.

"You'll like that. Dan's a good fisherman. And he is a good friend too."

*****

"What's this thing about a care group?" Brian asked a few weeks later. "They mentioned it in church, and Dan said I should come to the one at your place."

"It's a group of people who get together every week or two to study the Bible together, pray, and talk about our lives," John said. "It's a group of people who take care of each other. That's why it's called a care group. We meet Wednesdays at seven. You're absolutely welcome to come. You should come."

*****

The Smyths' living room was festooned on all sides with pine boughs and Christmas decorations. A large Christmas tree stood in front of the picture window, making the room even more crowded than usual.

"What's with all the decorations? It's only the first week of December," Angelo Moscatelli complained. "There's hardly enough room in here for us." Angelo was a round man with big smile and a black handlebar mustache.

"What can I say?" John Smyth answered. "Ruby loves Christmas. There are a lot of decorations here, but we'll always make room for an Angelo Elf."

Angelo beamed. "An Angelo Elf the size of Santa Claus."

John looked around at the group. "Since we have some new people here tonight, perhaps we should introduce ourselves," he said. "But briefly. The last time I asked this group to tell their stories, they talked about themselves for two hours. They went on and on."

"There was a lot to tell," Angelo said.

Everyone laughed.

"I'll start and show you how it's done," John said. "I grew up here in Winnipeg. I went to Grace Bible College and Seminary in Medicine Hat, Alberta, and then came back here and became editor of *Grace* magazine, denominational magazine of the Grace Evangelical Churches of North America. See, short and simple."

"That's because you are short and simple and you have lived a boring life" Angelo said. "There wasn't much to tell."

Everyone laughed.

"I grew up on a farm near Swift Current, Saskatchewan," Ruby said. "I also went to Grace Bible College, where I met John. We got married, and he brought me here to the big city. And now we have three wonderful children...and Michael."

"The group laughed again.

"What's with Michael?" Brian asked.

John hesitated. "Well, Michael is...How should I say it?...Michael is a teenager."

Angelo nodded. "It is a good thing your children are at the kids club and youth group tonight and he did not hear you say that."

"Michael is well aware that he is a teenager," John said. "We've discussed it several times."

"I'll go next," Dan said. "I'm a fisherman."

`   "And you also work forty hours a week as an auto mechanic," John said.

"Sure," Dan said. "But that's just a hobby. My calling is fishing."

"I can assure you that's true," Martha said. "I am a caretaker. I am responsible for taking care of Fisherman Dan."

"That is more than a forty-hour-a-week job," Ruby suggested.

"You're telling me," Martha agreed.

"Tell us about yourself, Brian," John said.

"There's very little to tell," Brian said. "I grew up in Calgary. I was an only child, and my parents were killed in an accident when I was twenty. I got a job working at a print shop in Calgary and moved here a few months ago. I work at Best Press now."

"Do you have any other family?" Martha asked.

"No. I've never been married, and I don't have any children."

John turned to the thirtyish woman in the stylish green dress on the other side of the room. She had short, dark hair, stylishly cut. "And you, Audrey?" John asked.

She flashed a brief smile. "I am an accountant and a widow. I have no children. My husband died two years ago."

*****

"I wish you hadn't been so insistent on everyone being brief," Ruby said that evening. "I would have liked to know more, particularly about Brian and Audrey."

"I agree with you," John said. "I'm sorry I said that too. It was just that last time everyone got carried away. Of course, Brian never says much about his past anyway."

"Maybe it's too hard, remembering his parents," Ruby suggested. "Some of his memories must be painful."

"Yes," John said, "but I think there might be more to it than that. And Audrey didn't reveal much either."

"Same thing. Her memories aren't all pleasant either," Ruby said. "But you could have said more too. You never challenged Angelo's assertion that your life is boring."

"How could my life be boring being married to you?" John asked.

"I'm delightful, I know," Ruby said, "but that's not what I was talking about."

"You mean that I have accidentally gotten involved in a couple of murder investigations?"

"Yes."

"No one needs to know about that."

*****

The care group was gathered again in the Smyth living room.

"Before we get started, I think we should all thank John and Ruby for welcoming us into their home every week," Reuben said. "You two clearly have the gift of hospitality."

"You have that backwards," John said. "We are blessed to have good friends who want to come to our house. You have given us the gift of friendship."

"Of course, you would say that," Reuben countered. "It's Ruby who does all the hosting work."

"That's true," John said.

Everyone laughed.

"But I really am grateful to be here," Brian said. "This is a very welcoming home."

"That reminds me," Angelo said. "I keep forgetting to ask. Where do you live, Brian?"

"In the Toba Tower."

"Really?" Angelo asked. "In that experimental green building the government keeps bragging about? What's it like?"

"It's actually pretty good," Brian said. "The place is so well built, so well insulated, that even though it's in the middle of the city, I don't hear anything, no traffic noise, nothing from the other units."

"I would hate that," Ruby said. "It's all the noises from outside that remind us that we are not alone."

"The solitude is really very peaceful," Brian said.

"Is it as environmentally friendly as the government says? Does that really work?" Angelo asked.

"It does," Brian said. "As I said, the building is so well insulated that the heat exchangers don't have to work very hard. You just set the climate controls and let the electronics do the rest. You can even set different temperatures for different rooms. You can keep the bedrooms cool for sleeping or warm if you prefer that."

"That's a pretty expensive place to live isn't it?" Angelo persisted.

"Well, there's quite a variety of units. There are the penthouses on the top floor. And some units have three bedrooms and a den, and others are smaller. I have one of the smallest units, a small one-bedroom. The utility costs are very low, and the government paid to install the heat exchanger system, so that kept the upfront cost down."

*****

The care group was assembled again. It was late January, in the middle of a bleak Winnipeg winter, Brian's second winter in the city.

"Before we start tonight, Brian has something to tell you," John said. "Brian?"

Brian took a deep breath. "I have been coming to this care group for a little over a year. I want to tell you that I have been talking to Pastor Young, and I'm going to be baptized in a few weeks. I have become a Christian."

"That's wonderful!" Angelo exclaimed.

"I need to tell you that it wasn't primarily because of John's teaching that convinced me."

"No kidding!" Angelo said.

"It's because of all of you. It's one thing to talk about the love of God, but you showed me the love of God. When I came to Winnipeg, I didn't have any friends, and I didn't know if I would make any. But now I'm surrounded by friends. You're like family."

*****

"This is scary," Brian said.

Pastor Young put his arm around Brian and said, "I know. I have to do it every week."

The congregation laughed.

"Just tell your story," the pastor said.

"I had a normal childhood, I guess. I didn't have any brothers or sisters. I had good parents. At least, they took care of me, but they didn't talk to me much. We never went to church. I never had a purpose or goal in life. I just sort of drifted. I did okay in school, but I didn't have any close friends. My parents died in a car crash when I was twenty and just finishing college. I think I just became numb after that. I got a job, but I didn't have any family or friends. I just sort of existed. Then, about a year and a half ago, I moved to Winnipeg to take another job. I didn't expect that to change much, but it changed everything. Shortly after I moved here, John Smyth invited me to dinner. Then I got invited to come to church, to go to the men's group, and to join John and Ruby's care group. It was astounding. I was suddenly surrounded by people who loved me and cared about me. I had never experienced that before. It changed everything. They were people who had a purpose and direction. I wondered what made them the way they are. And that's when I discovered Jesus. Like them, I now have a personal relationship with Jesus. And that's why I want to be baptized today, to show that I am a follower of Jesus too."

*****

"John, can I talk to you?" Brian asked.

They were standing on the steps of the church after service.

"Sure, Brian. What's up?"

"I was wondering if you could talk to Angelo. Ever since I was baptized, he has been pushing me to ask Audrey out."

"Angelo can certainly be pushy," John agreed. "But it's not a bad idea. Audrey's a good woman."

"Oh, I know," Brian said. "Audrey's very attractive. But I wouldn't want to...um...it wouldn't be fair to her."

"Audrey's stronger than you think," John said. "She and her first husband were only married seven years. They met at university. The first three years were good, but then Oscar got cancer. Audrey took care of him for four years and at the same time supported both of them. She was a full-time caregiver while starting her career. She is a remarkable woman. Oscar's been gone for three years, and she deserves a good husband."

"I agree. I agree," Brian said. "But I can't be that for her. It wouldn't be..."

Brian walked away before John could question him further.

*****

"Hi, John. It's Brian."

"Oh, hi, Brian," John said into the phone. "What's up?'

"I wanted to let you know that I won't be at church on Sunday or at care group. I have to go away."

"Where?"

"Um...Calgary. I have an aunt who's dying, and there isn't anyone else left to help her."

"How long will you be gone?"

"I don't know. Two or three weeks, maybe. I'll see how it goes."

"Is there anything we can do?"

"Well, I wondered if you would be willing to keep an eye on my place, collect the mail, and water the plants."

John smiled. "Sure, I would be glad to. Is there anything else you need?"

"No, not really."

"Okay. We'll pray for you and your aunt."

174

Chapter 2

The body was half sitting, half lying, propped against the pillows on the king size bed. The taut, bronzed skin was stretched tightly over the bone structure.

"That *is* a human body?" Detective Devorkian asked. He was tall and athletic and immaculately dressed in a three-piece, dark blue, pin stripe suit.

"Yes. It's too early for Halloween pranks." Isaac Laslo, the coroner, encased in scrubs, gloves, and a mask, did not look up from his work.

"Cause of death?" Devorkian asked.

"Too early to tell. Possibly that," Laslo said, indicating a discoloration in the center of the forehead.

"Any idea how long he has been dead?"

"Months," Laslo said.

Devorkian nodded and stepped out of the room. Sergeant Hosschuk was a little shorter and stockier, with unruly blond hair. His brown sports coat was unbuttoned. He wore no tie.

"Who found the body?" Devorkian asked.

"Technician named Axel Martin. He's inspecting and servicing all of the heat exchanger equipment in the building," Hosschuk said.

"Where is he?"

"Probably on the third floor. I said he could keep working, but not on this floor. I thought he should stay close by if you wanted to talk to him. I have his cell phone number."

*****

Axel Martin was a middle-aged man, about twenty pounds overweight. He was wearing dark green pants, a lighter green shirt with a GreenTech logo over the pocket and a matching logo on his cap.

"Mr. Martin, I'm Detective Devorkian. I understand you found the body in unit 212?"

"It was a body?"

"Oh, yes."

"I thought so, it didn't look quite real, but it still didn't look right, so I called the cops."

"Can you tell me what you were doing when you found the body?"

"Sure. This building has an innovative high-tech heat exchanger system installed by my company. It's top of the line, practically runs itself. It has a built-in monitoring system, but we're required to do a visual inspection every two years. So, I start on the first floor and work my way up to the second."

"How did you gain access to the units?"

"I knock on the door. If someone's home, they let me in. If not, I call the super, who uses his pass key."

"Did you need to call him often?"

"About half the time. He's mostly just hanging about, not far away."

"How long does it take you in each unit?"

"Ten minutes? I do a visual inspection and check the filters."

"Tell me about unit 212. Did you need the super to let you in?"

"Oh, yeah. I knocked. No one answered. He let me in."

"Then what?"

"There's a main unit in the living room and secondary units in every other room. I check the main unit, all good. I go into the first bedroom, first thing I notice it's ice cold, and the fan's blowing full blast."

"Cold?"

"Yeah. I figure something must have gone wrong with the unit. I go over, and I see the thermostat's set at three degrees Celsius. That's nuts. I look around, and there he is."

"You didn't see him when you first went into the room?"

"No. Drapes are closed, and the lights are off. I felt the cold before I hit the light switch. I'm focused on the exchanger to see what's wrong. I turn down the fan, change the setting, and it starts pumping out heat. I turn around, and that's when I see the body. I get the heck out and call 911." Martin hesitated. "Um...Was it the cold that killed him?"

"We don't know yet, but probably not," Devorkian said. "I would be surprised if your company's equipment was responsible, but it's too early to say for sure." He paused. "When was the last time you were here?"

"I'd have to check my records," Martin said. "Building's been open four years. We're supposed to check it every two years, so probably July two years ago."

"And you haven't been back since?"

Martin shook his head. "Nope."

"Could you call the super and ask him to come here?" Devorkian said.

*****

A thin man with white hair and a white mustache was coming down the hall. He was formally dressed in black dress pants, a white shirt, and a black bow tie.

Devorkian stopped him. "Are you the super?"

"I am the manager," the man said stiffly. "The Toba Tower is a high-end condo tower, not some low-rent apartment building. Buildings such as this one have a manager, not a superintendent. Now, if you will excuse me. I am needed by a technician who is on a service call."

Devorkian stopped the man again. "Axel Martin does not need you at the moment. I do. I asked him to call you here. I am Detective Devorkian, and this is Sergeant Hosschuk. We are with the Winnipeg Police Department."

"Oh," the man said.

"What is your name, please?" Devorkian asked.

"Richard Roberts," the man said. "I suppose you are here about the tenant in unit 212. How can I help you?"

"I understand it was Mr. Martin who found the body," Devorkian said. "Did you also go into the unit?"

177

"No," Roberts said. "I let him into the unit and then left. He called and asked me to come back a few minutes later. When I arrived, Mr. Martin was back in the hallway and had called 911. When he got off the call, he explained that he had found that Mr. Peterson had apparently passed away in his bed. We agreed that we should close the door and leave the unit until the authorities arrived. I then went down to the front door to let them in."

"Mr. Peterson is the man who owns or rents the unit?"

"Owns. This is a condo tower, with the units occupied by the owners."

"What can you tell us about Mr. Peterson?" Devorkian asked. "What is his full name?"

"Bradley Peterson. He is an older gentleman, and he is an ideal resident. He always pays his condo fees on time. He has not broken any rules or caused any disturbance. I have never received a complaint about him, and he has never brought a complaint against any other owner. He is an exemplary owner." Roberts sighed. "It is just too bad it happened again."

"What do you mean again?" Devorkian asked.

"This is a highly sought after building, and there is very little turnover. The building has only been open for four years, but Mr. Peterson is not the first owner. He moved in two years ago. The first owner of that unit had a heart attack. He managed to call 911. I was on duty and let the paramedics in when they arrived. There was an investigation, and the records show that they arrived within twenty minutes. Unfortunately, Mr. Bronwen died on the way to the hospital. Two deaths in the same unit might make it harder to sell."

"I don't think the deaths are connected," Devorkian said.

"People won't necessarily believe that."

"How many units have been resold?" Devorkian asked.

"Just five in four years, but two on this floor," Roberts said. "That's far below what's common for other buildings. City dwellers move every five years on average."

"When was the last time you saw Mr. Peterson?" Devorkian asked.

"Oh, I can't say," Roberts said. "I don't keep track of the residents. They are free to come and go, you know. I don't recall the last time I saw Mr. Peterson."

"What do you know about Mr. Peterson?"

"We don't pry into the owners' lives. We only know what they volunteer to tell us."

"And what did Mr. Peterson volunteer? Do you know if he has family nearby? Do you have records of next of kin, emergency contact numbers?"

"Oh, no, nothing like that." Roberts paused. "Well, only if they volunteer the information. Some buildings do that, but it is not a legal requirement. In the Toba Tower, we highly value the owners' privacy."

"Does the building have security cameras?" Devorkian asked.

"Outside, in the underground parking garage, and in the front lobby, but not in the interior of the building. We have assured the residents that we will protect their privacy. That's why we erase the tapes after a month."

"A month?" Devorkian sighed. "Does Mr. Peterson have a car?"

"Yes, down in the underground parking. I'll have to look up which parking slot is his. I can also give you the make and license plate number."

*****

"Unbelievable," Devorkian muttered as they walked away. "He knows more about the man's car than he does about the man himself. He thinks Bradley Peterson is the ideal resident because he hasn't caused any trouble. He didn't cause any trouble because he's been dead for months—and as far as he knows, the man could have been dead for two years."

"You know what they say," Hosschuk answered. "In any investigation, the first twenty-four months are crucial."

179

Devorkian scowled. "Twenty-four hours, not months."

Hosschuk agreed. "I know, and we're way behind. What are you thinking?"

"Mostly, I have a lot of questions. First off, do we even know that the body is Bradley Peterson? If it is, then why did no one notice he's been dead for months? Doesn't he have any friends or family? If he's been dead for months, who's paying his bills? And if it's not him, then who is it? And then where is Bradley Peterson? Did he kill the man on the bed and leave him there so we would think it was him and he could go into hiding?"

"Another question is: How did the killer get in?" Hosschuk said. "There was no sign of forced entry. Did he pick the lock? Climb up to the second floor balcony?"

"Maybe he just got a clipboard and a uniform like Martin has and knocked on the door."

"So, what do we do now?"

Devorkian thought for a moment. "I'm going to go down and look at Mr. Peterson's car. We should probably talk to all the other tenants and see if anybody saw anything or knows anything. Why don't you start with that?"

*****

Richard Roberts led Devorkian across the dimly lit floor of the underground parking garage.

"There it is in the corner," Roberts said, pointing. "Slot 118."

Devorkian walked over and circled the car. It was a late model gold Lexus with a layer of dust on it.

"Beautiful car," Roberts said.

"It is," Devorkian agreed.

*****

"Did you find the car?" Hosschuk asked.

"Yes. It's a Lexus, maybe three years old, expensive model," Devorkian said. "The dealer plate says it was bought in Calgary. The license tag expired last summer. It's covered in dust and obviously hasn't been driven in some time. We'll have to have it towed and have forensics go over it when they're finished in the apartment. How is the door to door going?"

"About what you would expect. Half the people aren't home. The other half don't recall seeing Peterson and don't know anything about him."

*****

It was late in the day when forensics had finished their work and Devorkian and Hosschuk re-entered the unit. The front door opened into a long room leading to a wall of outside windows. To their left was a treadmill, and ahead of them was a living room and dining room.

"Forensics have looked for the fine details—fingerprints, fibers, and so on," Devorkian said. "I want to look at the bigger picture. We need to find out who Peterson was, how he lived, and then how he died."

"Okay. Why would he put a treadmill in the living room right next to the front door?" Hosschuk asked.

"Perhaps because he almost never let anyone else into his unit," Devorkian answered. "Or maybe he didn't care what the place looked like. I never saw the point of treadmills anyway."

"Why?"

"It's just like running, but you never go anywhere and just stare at a wall. You put in all the work and get none of the fun."

They moved on into the living room, which consisted of a long couch on the right and a large television on the wall to the left with a long cabinet beneath it. The couch had recliner seats at each end.

"He has a lot of movies and video games," Hosschuk said, squatting to look through the long cabinet.

The "dining room" consisted of a small, round table with two chairs set against the wall of windows. To the right of

181

this was a galley kitchen with gleaming, stainless steel appliances behind a long island with a marble top. The two detectives looked through the cupboards and refrigerator.

"What do you think?" Devorkian asked.

"A well-stocked cupboard, but…"

"Precisely. Everything in the fridge and cupboards is in sealed containers—wine, beer, pop—but there are no perishables."

"He had a thing against fresh produce?" Hosschuk suggested.

"Think of the bedroom," Devorkian answered. "The killer set the thermostat to dehydrate the body, so it wouldn't be discovered for a long time and we would have trouble determining the time of death. I suspect the killer cleaned all the perishables out of the cupboard and fridge, so nothing would smell and attract attention."

"That's very methodical," Hosschuk said. "It suggests a very intelligent and methodical killer, maybe a professional hit."

"That's what I'm thinking."

They returned to the front door.

"Keys there on the hook by the door," Hosschuk observed.

To the right of the door was a coat closet and then a hall. They turned down the hall. There was a bathroom to the left and a linen and storage closet to the right. At the end of the hall were doorways leading left and right. They went in through the one on the left, which was the master bedroom. It was the room where the body had been found.

After a while, Devorkian asked, "Find anything? Impressions?"

"A decent set of clothes. Some books. A TV on the wall opposite the bed. Nothing remarkable as far as I can tell. Forensics said his watch and his wallet with ID and credit cards were in the drawer of the side table. They took them for processing. His cell phone was also on the bedside table, and they took that too."

"There's also nothing remarkable in the master bathroom," Devorkian said. "Some blood pressure and prostate meds."

Hosschuk shrugged. "What we might expect for a man his age."

They crossed the hall to the other room. It was dominated by a large mahogany desk. The walls were lined with bookshelves.

"Interesting mix of books," Devorkian said after a while. "A lot of science and technology, some business manuals, some history and biography, a few novels."

"But no records," Hosschuk said.

"Probably all on the computer," Devorkian said. "It's likely password protected. We'll have to take it to tech too and see if they can unlock it."

"There's this. It was in the righthand drawer of the desk," Hosschuk said, holding up a business card. "It looks like his accountant."

"Good," Devorkian said, looking at his watch. "It's too late to go there today. We'll go first thing in the morning." He leaned against the door frame to the office. "So, what do you think?"

Hosschuk sat back in the chair behind the desk. "Nice place."

"Nice?"

"Great place then. Efficient heating system. Lots of space. Good furniture."

"But what have we learned about Mr. Peterson? What's missing?"

"I don't know."

"No personal touches. No photographs."

"No address book," Hosschuk suggested.

"Possibly in the computer. But what did Peterson do here?"

Hosschuk considered. "There's books, a television, video games...the treadmill..."

"That's it?"

Hosschuk shrugged. "You said we needed to find out who Peterson was and how he lived. I'm not sure we learned very much. What do we do now?"

"Let's grab those keys by the front door," Devorkian said.

They walked back down the hall.

"He certainly doesn't have a key to every door," Hosschuk said looking at the key ring. "Looks like two keys for the building, his unit and the outside door. And a car key. What's the little one?"

"My guess would be mailbox," Devorkian answered.

*****

They looked at the mail spread out on the desk.

"That's not a lot of mail to arrive in several months," Hosschuk said.

"There's no junk mail," Devorkian said.

"Could somebody have been picking it up?" Hosschuk asked.

"I don't think so. Look at this. A Christmas card from his insurance broker from two years ago, and another from last Christmas. And an invitation to a birthday party for someone named Carly from a year and a half ago."

"The rest are addressed to him, but they look like unsolicited mass mailings."

"Yes," Devorkian said. "He did not receive much mail. Tomorrow, we need to see his accountant, and then we need to talk to the mailman."

Chapter 3

Devorkian and Hosschuk walked through the front door of the four-story, glass and steel office complex and found themselves in a square reception area with a set of elevators straight ahead and large double doors on each side. The doors were guarded by twin reception desks. Bond and Bond Accounting Services was on the right.

"We're here to see Audrey Milner," Devorkian said to the middle-aged blonde receptionist.

"Do you have an appointment?" she asked.

"No," Devorkian answered.

When he said nothing further, the receptionist punched in a number and spoke into her headset. "Ms. Milner, there are two gentlemen here to see you. They did not give their names." She listened for a moment and said to Devorkian, "She will be here in a moment."

Audrey was immaculately dressed in a dark blue pant suit with a white blouse. She came out through the double doors and walked directly to the two men. "I'm Audrey Milner. How can I help you?"

Devorkian showed her his badge. "I am Detective Devorkian, and this is Sergeant Hosschuk, with the Winnipeg Police. Is there somewhere we could talk to you for a few moments?"

Audrey looked toward the receptionist, who said, "Meeting room three is available."

Audrey led them through the doors into a large room. The center was full of cubicles, while private offices lined the right and back walls. Venetian blinds on the office windows hid some of the occupants from view, while other blinds were open. Audrey led them to the third of a series of meeting rooms along the left wall. Inside was a wooden table surrounded by eight plush chairs. Audrey gestured to the chairs on one side of the table and sat down on the opposite side.

"Now, what do you have to tell me?" she said politely but curtly.

"Tell you?" Devorkian asked. "Why did you ask that?"

"When policemen come to see someone without advance warning, it usually means they are bringing bad news."

"Actually, we came to ask you to give us some information," Devorkian said.

"Okay, what do you want to know?"

"We found one of your business cards, "Devorkian said. "Is Bradley Peterson one of your clients?"

"He is," she answered after a moment. "But, by company policy, I cannot talk about a client's finances unless you have a warrant or a court order."

"It's a gray area," Devorkian said. "But client privilege does not apply in this case because Mr. Peterson died some months ago."

Audrey opened her mouth to speak, paused in thought for a moment, and said, "I'm sorry to hear that. But client privilege still exists with Mr. Peterson's heirs."

"You don't seem shocked to hear Mr. Peterson is dead," Devorkian observed. It was a question.

"You are not the first policemen I have encountered," she said. "As I said, when policemen show up, it usually means bad news."

"We believe Mr. Peterson might have been murdered, and we need to look at his financial records to help us find out who killed him. Surely, your responsibility to Mr. Peterson would include helping to solve his murder?"

Audrey nodded thoughtfully. "Just a moment." She stood, walked to a phone on a small table in the corner of the room, lifted the receiver, and punched in some numbers. "This is Audrey Milner. I'm in meeting room three. Could you see me for a quick consultation?" She listened, nodded, and hung up. "I'll be right back." She walked out into the main room, shutting the door behind her. The venetian blinds were open, and the detectives could see her standing there, obviously waiting.

A couple of minutes later, a man with prematurely gray hair and dressed in a closely fitted black suit came through the main door and approached her. They talked for a few minutes. Audrey nodded, and the man turned and walked back out through the main door. Audrey then walked over to the far side of the room and went in through an open door. She returned a few moments later carrying a black laptop computer, closed the door, sat back down across from the detectives, and opened the laptop.

"Bond and Bond is a unique organization," she said. "It is actually two fraternal organizations. Bond and Bond Accounting Services is an accounting firm. Bond and Bond Legal Services occupies the other half of this building. Because we work together, the two organizations can provide full legal and financial services to our clients. It is a very useful arrangement for situations such as this one. I just consulted with Mr. Silverthorne on the legal issues. He concurred with my assessment that I should not give you access to Mr. Peterson's financial records. We suggest that you get a warrant for that. However, since Mr. Peterson has signed a legal agreement allowing me to act on his behalf in certain limited circumstances, I will give you what assistance I can without violating client privilege."

"My first question is how Mr. Peterson could have been dead for several months without anyone noticing a problem with his finances," Devorkian said.

"That question occurred to me as well," Audrey said, "but then I realized it was perfectly possible."

"How?" Devorkian asked.

"I'll explain," Audrey said. "Mr. Peterson's accounts were transferred to us from our Calgary branch when he moved to Winnipeg about two years ago, and his financial accounts were assigned to me. You should understand that his finances are not complicated. They are quite straightforward. When we met, he explained that as much as possible he wanted his finances to be handled automatically. So, we set it up so that all of his bills—condo fees, property taxes, insurance, electric bill, phone bill, credit card bills, and so on—would be sent to him electronically, no paper. And we set it up so that those bills would be paid automatically from his checking account. He could check the bills as they came in, but they would be paid regardless of whether he did that or not. His condo and car are paid for, and he has no other debts. In the same way, his pension checks were deposited into the same checking account. He had retirement savings plans, but those had already been transferred into retirement investment funds, which paid a set amount into his checking account every month. He also has two tax-free savings accounts and another investment account. He received a fairly substantial monthly payment from another investment, and that money was automatically deposited into his investment account. He asked that I set up his accounts so that if his checking account ever reached a certain amount, money would be transferred from that account into his investment account, and if his checking account ever fell below a certain amount, money would be transferred into his checking account from his investment account."

"So, it was all done automatically, and he did not have to check on the accounts or do anything?" Devorkian asked.

"That's right. And I didn't have any need to look at the accounts either."

Devorkian thought for a moment. "What about his everyday spending, credit cards, and so on? Do you have access to those?"

"Yes, his credit cards are tied to his bank, so I can access those as well. As I said, Mr. Peterson signed an agreement giving me access to all of his accounts."

"Without showing them to me, could you have a look at them now?" Devorkian asked.

Audrey logged in to the laptop and began scrolling. After about five minutes, she stopped and sat back in her chair. "That's astounding," she said.

"What?" Devorkian asked.

"His expenditures, for food, groceries, whatever, were fairly steady and then suddenly stopped October 7."

"Last year?"

"No, the year before that."

"You mean, what, three months after he moved in?" Devorkian asked.

"Yes."

"He was dead for almost two years, his bills just kept getting paid, and nobody noticed?" Devorkian asked, incredulous.

"Apparently. According to these records, at least."

"What about his credit card? Wouldn't that have been canceled if there was no activity for that long?"

"No, because he routed some of his monthly bills to be paid through his credit cards, so he could get the points."

"What about his income taxes? He would have to file those."

Audrey smiled and tilted her head. "Remember that he gave me access to his accounts? He had instructed me to look at his income and deductions and file his income tax returns for him. A lot of people do that. I did that for him the last two years. The arrangement we had was that I would email him a copy and if he didn't respond with any comments or questions, I would file the returns. He did not want to be bothered unless there was a problem. He did not comment either year, so I filed his returns. The refunds were automatically deposited into his checking account."

"Astounding," Devorkian said. "What about his family? Do you know if he had any family and how to reach them?"

"No," Audrey said. Then she smiled. "For that, you would be better asking his lawyer. I told Mr. Silverthorne that you would likely want to talk to him when we were finished here."

Audrey stood and led them back out into the reception area. She approached the receptionist at the desk on the opposite site of the space.

"These gentlemen are here to see Mr. Silverthorne," she said. "I believe he is expecting them."

The receptionist punched some buttons and then spoke into her headset. "Mr. Silverthorne, there are two gentlemen here to see you. I believe you are expecting them." She turned to the two detectives with a bureaucratic smile on her face. "He will be with you shortly."

A few moments later, the man with prematurely gray hair and the closely fitted black suit came through the main door and approached the detectives. "Come this way," he said.

Silverthorne led them back through the doorway he had just come from. Inside was a layout that was a mirror image of the office they had just left—meeting rooms to the right, private offices along the left and rear walls, and junior employees busily toiling in cubicles in the center. Silverthorne led them to a private office along the right wall.

"I am Arthur Silverthorne," he said as he moved behind a large oak desk and turned to face them. "And you are?"

"Detective Devorkian and Sergeant Hosschuk of the Winnipeg Police," Devorkian said.

"Please sit down," Silverthorne said, indicating two plush chairs in front of the desk, while he himself sat in a high-backed leather chair behind the desk. "I understand that you are here about a man named Bradley Peterson, who is a client of ours?"

"Yes," Devorkian said.

"We had not heard about his death," Silverthorne said. "Could you tell me when he died, and is there a death certificate?"

"According to your accounting colleague in the other office, it is likely that he died in early October more than a year and a half ago."

"Oh, my," said Silverthorne. "Why haven't we been informed before this?"

"Because his body was not found until yesterday. There is no death certificate because we are still investigating the circumstances of his death."

Silverthorne was thoughtful. "That means he likely died only a few months after he moved here and not long after I saw him. He seemed in good health then."

"We think he might have been murdered," Devorkian said. "It would be helpful if you could give us as much information as possible in order to determine who might have wanted to kill him."

Silverthorne pulled a sheet of paper out of a file on his desk and slid it over to Devorkian. "I don't know if you have this information, but I believe these are his closest relatives. Anne Ravari was his wife, but they divorced some years ago, and the wife has remarried. The other two are his son and daughter."

"Thank you," Devorkian said, looking over the paper.

"Do you know if the next of kin have been notified?" Silverthorne asked.

"Probably not, but we can do that," Devorkian said. "Do you know if Mr. Peterson had a will?"

"Yes, Mr. Peterson's account was transferred here from our Calgary office, and I prepared a new will for him. However, as you know, wills are private until after probate. If Mr. Peterson died almost two years ago and the body was found just now, I assume it would have been badly decomposed. Are you absolutely certain it is his body?"

Devorkian took a breath. "There is every indication that it is Mr. Peterson. Final confirmation will take some time, but I don't think there is much doubt."

"As I stated," Silverthorne said evenly, "wills are private until probate. I am afraid I cannot allow you to see it until probate."

Devorkian said, "I understand lawyer-client privilege. On the other hand, you have a duty to act in the best interests of your client. At this point, the evidence suggests that he was murdered. As a lawyer, you should want to do whatever you can to assist the police in finding out who killed your client."

Silverthorne smiled. "You should have been a lawyer, detective. Legally, I cannot show you the will until after probate. However, you could get a court order to see the will, and I would be glad to comply when that happens. I suggest you do that. In the meantime, I will do what I can. I have given you the names and contact information of the next of kin. As well, I can say, in a general sense, that there is nothing in the will that would suggest a motive to commit murder."

"Are you saying that Mr. Peterson's estate is not very valuable?" Devorkian demanded.

"No, I am not saying that. Mr. Peterson had an estate that I would describe as considerable, not massive but considerable. However, no one would benefit greatly from it."

"I am not sure I understand," Devorkian said.

Silverthorne took another breath. "In my opinion, Mr. Silverthorne left an amount to each of his family members that was considerable but not life-changing. I might add that he had a preference for round numbers."

Devorkian considered that. "So, we're thinking somewhere in the neighborhood of, say, a hundred thousand each?"

"I can neither confirm nor deny that," Silverthorne said with a smile. "I suggest you get a court order."

"What about the rest of his estate?" Devorkian asked.

Silverthorne took another deep breath. "I can say that the bulk of Mr. Peterson's estate is likely to go as a charitable donation to a large institution, an institution which can function very well without Mr. Peterson's gift. In my opinion, you would be wasting your time to pursue that line of inquiry."

"To your knowledge, are Mr. Peterson's beneficiaries aware of the contents of his will?"

"I have no way of knowing that," Silverthorne said. "As I said, wills are private until probate. But whether Mr. Peterson shared that information with his beneficiaries I cannot tell you."

"Thank you, Mr. Silverthorne," Devorkian said, rising. "You have been...helpful."

"I do what I can," Silverthorne said. "I would appreciate it if you would let me know when you have the identity of the deceased confirmed and when a death certificate has been issued. Then I will be able to contact the beneficiaries and begin work on sorting out his estate."

"Are you his executor?" Devorkian asked sharply.

"Administrator," Silverthorne said. "Lawyers do not act as executors."

*****

"I would say that was helpful on the whole," Hosschuk said.

"At least, we have something to go on," Devorkian agreed. "I'd like you to go back to the Toba Tower and finish talking to the neighbors. Also, talk to the person who delivers the mail. There's something off about that. See if you can find out what happened to the rest of his mail."

"And what will you be doing?"

"I'm going to check in with Laslo for the autopsy results. Tomorrow, I will be catching an early flight out to Calgary, where Peterson's family members live."

"You're going to inform the next of kin in person? Usually, we would ask the Calgary Police to do that."

"I'm hoping they will tell me more than I tell them. We need to know a lot more about Mr. Peterson if we hope to figure out who would want to kill him."

"Okay. I can't argue with that." Hosschuk scratched his cheek. "Something about what we heard is bothering me. October almost two years ago—why does that sound familiar?"

"The Air Canada crash," Devorkian said.

"Right. I remember," Hosschuk said. "Not our case."

"No, but they wanted our help tracking down one of the passengers, a man named Ryan Scott. They knew he flew in two days earlier and back out on October 10. It was a false name, and they were never able to identify him. They thought he might be a terrorist and might be responsible for the crash. They wanted us to find out what Scott did in the two days he was here."

"Total waste of time," Hosschuk said. "We spent months working on that and found nothing, and in the end it didn't matter. They ruled the crash was due to mechanical failure and Scott, whoever he was, had nothing to do with it."

"Let's hope we are more successful with this case," Devorkian said. "I hate unsolved cases."

*****

"What can you tell me?" Devorkian asked.

"No real surprises," Laslo said. "He was shot once, in the center of the forehead. He would have died very quickly."

"Did you recover the bullet?"

"No."

"No?"

"It must have been a fairly large caliber. How large is difficult to say, given the shrinkage of the body. The bullet passed through the skull. Forensics think it then passed through the pillow and into the headboard."

"So, did forensics recover the bullet?" Devorkian asked.

"They say not. Their conclusion is that it was dug out of the headboard. It was lucky for the killer that he was able to do that."

"I'm not sure it was luck," Devorkian said. "We think this might have been a professional hit. A professional could have lined up the victim in front of the pillow and headboard so he could recover the bullet." He paused. "Anything else you can tell me?"

"For an older man, he was relatively healthy. Everything else will have to wait for lab tests."

*****

The mailboxes were in a small room off the lobby of the Toba Tower. Sally Whittaker, a middle-aged, slightly overweight brunette, was efficiently sorting mail into the slots when she suddenly stopped and looked around hesitantly. She froze when she saw the stocky man in the rumpled brown suitcoat. He was standing against the wall in the lobby watching her.

She turned toward him. "Do you want something?"

"Not yet. You can finish what you are doing," Hosschuk replied.

When she had finished and had slammed the big cover shut on all the mailboxes, he stepped forward. He held up

194

his badge. "I am Detective Sergeant Hosschuk with the Winnipeg Police. I have some questions for you."

She started to push past him. "I need to finish my route. The mail should not be delayed."

He put out a hand in front of her to stop her. "We can talk here, or we can go down to the police station and have an official interrogation."

She hesitated. "Fine."

"We can talk in your truck if you like," Hosschuk said, nodding to the post office vehicle parked outside by the main entrance.

"What can you tell me about Bradley Peterson in unit 212?" Hosschuk asked when they were seated in the truck.

"I don't know anything about him. I just put the mail into the right boxes. I look at the unit number more than the names."

"That is not entirely true," Hosschuk said. "I saw you hesitate. You realized Mr. Peterson's box was empty for the first time in months."

"I hesitated because I saw you standing there staring at me. That's harassment."

"Let me tell you something," Hosschuk said. "I don't care about the mail, but I need to know about Mr. Peterson. He has been murdered, and you had better tell me what you know before I charge you with obstruction."

"Murdered?!" she exclaimed. "I didn't know. That's got nothing to do with me. I just deliver the mail."

"Mr. Peterson was murdered months ago, and, in all that time, you have been delivering mail to him, but his box remained relatively empty. Why?"

Sally Whittaker burst into tears. "I didn't know. I could lose my job. We are required to deliver the mail."

"I don't care about any of that," Hosschuk said solemnly. "Just tell me the truth, and it doesn't have to go any further. I won't tell your superiors."

"You won't?" she said tearfully.

"No, I won't, but you are going to have to tell me the truth."

She took a deep breath. "It was almost two years ago. I was sorting the mail like I was today, and this man approached. I didn't know who he was, but he said he was Mr. Peterson from unit 212. He said he didn't want any junk mail put into his box. I said I was just an employee and we were required to put those things into everyone's box."

"That's not entirely true, is it?" Hosschuk said. "People can put a note on their box asking that no advertising be put in."

"Yes," she admitted. "But that only applies to advertising. Other things, like government mass mailings, still have to be put in, and he didn't want even that."

"You didn't want to be bothered."

She sighed. "It's extra work having to decide what goes in and what doesn't...I explained all that to him."

"But he didn't accept that?"

"He asked what he could do to change it, and I said nothing. And then...then..."

"Then what?"

"He said he would pay me a hundred dollars a month not to put any unaddressed mail into his box. My car had just broken down, and I needed money to repair it. He..."

"He what?"

"He handed me a thousand dollars on the spot."

Hosschuk smiled. "So, you stopped putting unaddressed mail into his box? Then what?"

"Then nothing. I didn't put any of those things into his box, but I continued to deliver the addressed mail. For a while, he picked up his mail regularly, but after a couple of months he stopped. I never saw him again. I didn't know what to do. I couldn't report it, or I would get into trouble, so I just continued..."

Chapter 4

The house was a full two stories with a basement, baby blue vinyl siding, and large windows trimmed in white. It was a new house in a new subdivision. A circular driveway large enough to hold half a dozen cars had been carved into a green lawn. Devorkian stepped onto the low front step beneath a peaked roof supported by white classical columns. He pushed the doorbell button. The door was opened by a woman of medium height. Her short, dark hair had streaks of gray. She was dressed in a stylish, blue pantsuit.

"Mrs. Anne Ravari?" Devorkian asked.

"Yes," she answered warily.

"I am Detective Devorkian," he said, holding up his badge. "May I come in and talk to you for a few minutes?"

She hesitated a moment before opening the door wider and ushering him into a beautifully furnished living room.

"I am with the Winnipeg Police Department," he said when they had sat down on opposite cream plush couches. "There is no easy way to say this. I am sorry to have to tell you that your former husband, Bradley Peterson, has been found dead."

"Oh," she said.

"His body was found in his condo on Monday, but he had apparently been dead for some time. We are trying to discover the circumstances surrounding his death and why he was not discovered right away. I was hoping that you could shed some light onto the type of man he was, his background, and so on."

"Oh," she said again.

"Is there anything you can tell me?"

She took a deep breath. "Well, Bradley was about ten years older than me. He was an only child, his mother died of cancer when he was still a boy, and his father committed suicide when he was eighteen. He inherited their house and quite a lot of money. He used the money to buy his business."

"What business?"

"Fast Eddy's Printing. He was a good businessman. It was just a small shop and not doing well when he bought it, and he grew it into the largest print shop in the city."

"I see. Go on."

"I was nineteen when we got married. I was working in a coffee shop, and Bradley would come in all the time. He was pleasant, not pushy like a lot of the customers. I was looking for stability and security, I think. Bradley was a good provider. We dated for a few months and then got married. The first years I was happy for the most part, but the marriage soon cooled."

"Was Bradley unfaithful?"

She shook her head. "Not as far as I know. I doubt it. It wasn't that. Bradley was not very expressive or demonstrative. Maybe it was because of his upbringing, growing up without a mother, and I think his father didn't pay much attention to him either. Anyway, as time went on, Bradley seemed to withdraw more and more. He was not abusive or angry. He just became distant. His business was very demanding, and he often ate supper at the office or at a restaurant near the office and then went back to work. When he did come home, after supper he would go into his office here. He said he had been around people all day and needed a break from that. We didn't quarrel. He wasn't around enough for that. I think I had known for some time what I would do. I started taking some courses and eventually was certified as a nurse's aid. I went back to work, part-time at first and then full-time, and eventually upgraded to a full nursing degree. By that time, the kids were grown and moving out of the house, so I told Bradley I wanted a divorce. He didn't get angry or argue. He didn't fight. He didn't even try to save our marriage. I think that was the most disappointing thing about it, but I should have expected it by then. I'd known what he was like for a long time. He just moved out. The divorce was uncontested. He gave me the house and my car, and a cash settlement. There was no alimony because I was working and didn't need it."

"May I ask what the cash settlement was?" Devorkian asked. "Was it perhaps something like a hundred thousand dollars?"

"Why, yes," she said. "How did you know?"

"Just a guess," Devorkian answered. "We have managed to learn a little about how Bradley approached things. Is there anything else you can tell me?"

She shrugged. "I pretty much just forgot about Bradley and moved on. I wasn't planning to remarry after my first marriage had been so disappointing. In reality, I had been managing on my own for quite a long time. But then I met Javon about five years ago, and we got married. It was a good decision. He was a widower. I sold my house and put the money into savings. This was Javon's house."

"When was the last time you talked to Bradley?"

"Oh, years. He sent the children a change of address notice when he moved to Winnipeg, but he didn't send me one. I don't remember the last time I talked to him or even heard from him. We have no reason to communicate." She sighed. "I don't hate him, you know. I feel sorry for him really. He cut himself off from everyone. I think it was harder on the children."

"You have two children?"

"Yes, David and Angela."

"I would like to talk to them as well. I have addresses for them. Do you think they would be at home this morning?"

"Angela should be, but you would probably find David at Calgary General Hospital. He's an ER doctor."

"One final question. We are not sure about the circumstances of Bradley's death. There is a possibility of foul play. Do you know of anyone who would want to harm or kill Bradley?"

Anne sat back and sucked in her breath. "Do you mean he was murdered?"

"It is one possibility. The investigation is still in its early stages. Do you know of anyone who would want to hurt him? Did he quarrel with anyone or offend someone? Could anyone have had a grudge against him?"

"No, certainly not," Anne said. "You need to understand. Bradley was...uninvolved. He didn't inspire love or hate. Most people were indifferent to him."

The waiting room was crowded, most of the couple of dozen chairs were filled, and a few people were standing, leaning on walls. Devorkian surveyed the scene. Along one wall was a queue of people waiting to approach one of the two check-in desks. Devorkian stood beside the queue, and when one of the check-in desks came free, he strode forward, held up his badge, and said quietly, "I won't take much of your time. I am Detective Devorkian, and I need to see Dr. David Peterson. Is he working today?"

The clerk, a middle-aged woman with curly brown hair, hesitated. She picked up a telephone handset, punched in some numbers, and spoke quietly into the set. "Dr. Peterson will come when he is finished with his current patient," she said to Devorkian after hanging up. She indicated a set of double wooden doors to the right of the check-in desks.

Devorkian thanked her and moved over to stand about ten feet in front of the doors, far enough back not to be in the way and close enough not to be missed.

About ten minutes later, a tall, thin man came through the doors. He was wearing dark pants, a white shirt, and a white lab coat. He was clean-shaven with short, brown hair.

Devorkian approached him. "Dr. Peterson? I am Detective Devorkian of the Winnipeg Police. Is there somewhere where we could talk in private for a few minutes?"

Peterson looked around and then led the way through a set of doors on the other side of the room and into a hallway. About twenty feet away, the hallway widened into another small waiting room. Only a handful of people were sitting there, and Peterson led the way to the back corner. "Will this do?" he asked.

"Yes, thank you," Devorkian said as they sat in plastic chairs facing each other. "Dr. Peterson, it is my sad duty to inform you that your father, Bradley Peterson, has passed away."

Peterson shrugged one shoulder, stretched his neck to the side, and took a deep breath. "These kinds of conversations are a difficult part of our jobs. I have been on the other side and know how difficult they are. Thank you for telling me." He paused. "How did he die?"

"That is still under investigation. Your father was found deceased in his condo, and it appears he had been dead for some months before he was found. Can you tell me when you were last in touch with your father?"

Peterson let out a long breath. "That would have been at least two years ago. He sent me a change of address notice when he moved to Winnipeg, and it was before that that we talked, on the phone, I think. I don't really remember. Our interactions were usually brief."

"You don't seem very upset to hear that your father has died. What can you tell me about him?"

Peterson was quiet for a moment. "I mourned for my father a long time ago. He moved out of my life years ago, if he ever was in my life. That's not entirely true. I have vague memories of him playing with us when I was quite young. But, as time went on, he was around less and less, and he rarely spoke to my sister and me. I'm not saying he was a bad father. He paid my way through medical school...but he never showed up for my graduation." David paused. "He gave money to me like he was paying another utility bill."

"You resent your father?"

"No, I don't think so anymore. I've accepted it. It was as if he died years ago. It is difficult growing up without a father. Sometimes, I felt like an orphan."

"But you grew up to have a successful career."

"True, but I can't say that my father contributed to that other than financially. I was fortunate."

"Fortunate?"

"Mom took really good care of us. She tried to make up for what we were missing out on. And then there was Baldy."

"Baldy?"

"Angelo Balducci. He was coach of the community soccer team, and he sort of took me under his wing. He also led a youth group at a church down the street from us. He was a surrogate father for me and for a lot of other boys in the neighborhood. Still, it took me a long time to get my head around the whole family thing."

"You're married?"

"Yes, and my wife has been very understanding." Peterson sighed. "We're expecting our first child in a few months, and it took some real soul-searching to decide that's what I wanted to do. I wanted to be a better father than my father had been and wasn't sure I was up to it. I talked to Baldy about it, and he helped."

"Is there anything else you can tell me about your father?"

"I'm not sure. Like what?"

"Did he have any close friends who might know more about him?"

"No, he didn't seem to have any friends, at least any I knew of."

"What about enemies? Is there anyone he might have harmed financially or personally, anyone who might be angry with him, anyone who might have wanted to hurt him?"

"Why are you asking that? Are you saying my father was murdered?"

"As I said, his exact manner of death is still under investigation. We are looking at all possibilities. Did your father have any enemies? Can you think of anyone?"

"No, none that I know of." Peterson hesitated. "I wouldn't necessarily know. We were not that close."

"Why did you hesitate?" Devorkian demanded. "You thought of someone."

Peterson shrugged. "Well, Angela was...that is, all of us in the family were angry with him to one degree or another, but none of us would have done anything to harm him."

"Thank you for your time," Devorkian said. "Again, I am sorry about your father, and I'm sorry I had to bother you with questions."

Peterson shrugged. "I understand. It's your job. Sometimes, I have to ask uncomfortable questions in my job too."

"One more thing," Devorkian said. "We are quite certain that it was your father who was found in his condo. However, we have not been able to find any relatives or friends in Winnipeg who could positively identify the body."

Peterson hesitated.

"I'm not asking you to come to Winnipeg," Devorkian said. "But would you be willing to give me a DNA sample to compare to the deceased's?"

"Sure," Peterson said.

*****

The house was a small bungalow, with peeling white paint on the wooden siding and faded brown shutters beside the windows. Devorkian climbed five cement steps to a small landing and knocked on the door. After about a minute, it was opened by a woman in a white T-shirt and worn blue jeans. Her dark hair was tousled, and she wore no makeup.

"Angela Williams?" Devorkian asked.

"What do you want?" the woman asked warily.

Devorkian held up his badge. "I am Detective Devorkian. I need to talk with you. May I come in?"

She looked him over and then stepped back, allowing him to enter. "What's this about?"

"It would be better if we sat down," Devorkian said, gesturing toward the living room, where there were a couple of mismatched chairs and a worn, brown, corduroy couch. There were newspapers and books scattered on the end tables and children's toys scattered on the worn, green rug. The woman went over to a playpen in the corner and picked up a child who was standing at the railing staring at the stranger. She sat down on the couch with the child on her lap. She was holding him almost as a shield against whatever Devorkian might be bringing to her.

"I am with the Winnipeg Police," Devorkian said. "I have come to inform you that your father, Bradley Peterson, has passed away. I am very sorry."

Angela caught her breath and closed her eyes, leaning forward and hugging her child fiercely. A few sobs escaped her lips. It was the first grief over the death of Bradley Peterson that Devorkian had so far encountered.

"I am very sorry," Devorkian repeated after a few moments. "Would it be possible for me to ask you a few questions about your father?"

"I—I guess so," she said. "How did he die?"

"He was found passed away in his condo on Monday. We are still investigating the manner of his death. What can you tell me about your father?"

She took a deep breath. "What can I tell you? I loved my father, but I don't think my father ever loved me. My brother David said that he played with him when he was little, but I don't ever remember him playing with me. He was always working, and I hardly ever saw him. He never came to any school events. My mother did her best. She would organize big birthday parties for me and invite my friends, but my farther would only show up at the end and hand me an envelope with money in it. He would never even give me a hug or a kiss." Her voice broke. "I thought it might change when I had kids and gave him grandchildren. But he never even came when Markus and I got married, just sent some money. I would invite him to my kids' birthday parties, but he would never come. He would just mail me an envelope with a hundred dollars in it. When he moved to Winnipeg, he sent me a change of address card. I tried to phone him there a couple of times. Once, he didn't answer, and the other time, he just said hello and not much else. We were only on the phone a minute or two. I sent him an invitation to my daughter Carly's birthday party that fall, but he never responded, didn't even send money. It was clear he didn't love me and didn't want anything to do with me or my kids. After that, I just gave up."

"We have reason to believe that your father might not have received that invitation," Devorkian said softly. "We think he died within a couple of months of moving to Winnipeg."

"But how...? Why...?" At that point, she burst into tears.

Devorkian picked up a box of tissues from a side table and placed it on the coffee table in front of her. She snatched up a couple of tissues and rubbed furiously at her face. The child whimpered, and she hugged him tighter.

"I know it must be very upsetting to hear this," Devorkian said after a while. "But there is one more question I need to ask you."

"Yes?" she said in a weak voice.

"Do you know of anyone who had a grudge against your father, anyone who might have wanted to hurt him?"

"You..." She hesitated. "Are you saying that my father was murdered?"

"It is one possibility," Devorkian said. "As I said, the investigation is just beginning. Do you know of anyone who would want to harm him?"

"No," she said. "How could I? He never talked to me. I don't know anything about him or his business or who he knew in Winnipeg."

"One final question. You are married?"

"Yes. Markus is at work."

"What does he do?"

"He's a diesel mechanic."

"Does he share your...frustration with your father?"

"No. He doesn't care. He says we don't need my father's money, and I should just forget about him."

*****

The place was easy to find. The flashing neon image of a massive boy in blue and yellow was hard to miss, the churning legs indicating that this was Fast Eddy. It adorned the front unit of a two-story, light industrial complex.

Devorkian went in through the door to find a long counter. The interior walls were painted the same yellow as Fast Eddy's T-shirt. Two clerks, one male and one female, wearing yellow, two-button T-shirts with Fast Eddy logos over the breast pocket, were waiting on customers at the counter. Behind the counter were a number of other employees sitting at desks. As Devorkian entered, one of these jumped up and met him at the counter.

"Can I help you?"

"Yes. I would like to see the manager or owner, whoever is in charge," Devorkian said.

The clerk looked over Devorkian's stylish three-piece suit. "Just a moment." He turned, went back to his desk, picked up the phone, and spoke quietly for a few moments. Hanging up, he turned back to Devorkian. "Mr. Schmidt will be right out."

A few moments later, a tall, round man in a white shirt and tie came around a corner and up a passageway along one side of the counter space. He approached Devorkian.

"Rolly Schmidt," he said, extending a hand. "How can I help you."

"Could I speak to you in private?" Devorkian asked.

Schmidt led Devorkian back up the passageway and around a corner into a good-sized office. He motioned toward a set of comfortable chairs around a circular coffee table. "Please be seated. Now, how can I help you?"

Devorkian chose a chair and sat. "I am Detective Devorkian with the Winnipeg Police."

"Since I haven't been to Winnipeg for quite a number of years, I assume you are not here to arrest me. So, I'm glad to meet you."

"What can you tell me about Bradley Peterson?" Devorkian said.

"Why? What's Bradley got himself involved in now?"

"I will tell you that in a minute. First, I would appreciate it if you would answer my question. What do you know about him? What kind of man is he?"

"Well, when Bradley was sitting in this office, he was a strategic genius. You saw that Fast Eddy logo? Bradley designed that. Well, he came up with the idea and hired a good graphic designer to produce it. Then he spread that logo all over town. When you came in, did you have to wait long?"

"No, one of the people working at a desk jumped up and came over right away."

"Exactly. That was Bradley. There are customer reps at the counter, but Bradley came up with the idea that office staff would wait on customers when necessary, so there would be no waiting. Fast Eddy, you know?"

"Impressive."

"The print shop was not doing well when Bradley bought it, but he saw the potential. Location is key. It's just on the edge of downtown, with the city's main office towers just a couple of blocks away, and yet it was far enough away that the rent on a low-rise complex like this is more reasonable. And in the other direction is a major industrial section of the city. When Bradley bought this print shop, it only filled the first unit in this complex. Bradley arranged the lease so that it would be rent to own, and he slowly expanded the business one unit at a time. By the time he had expanded to fill the whole complex, he owned the whole building. Then he opened a new location next to the university. He's a genius."

"The staff liked him as a boss?"

"As I said, when Bradley was sitting in this office, he was a strategic genius. He is not so good outside of this office. He does not like people."

"Did that create problems with the staff?"

"This shop pays the best wages in the city. The staff got big bonuses at Christmas, a form of profit sharing. But there was no Christmas party, no personal touch. For the most part, the staff were happy with their jobs, but they almost never saw Bradley."

"If he did not like to go out and meet people, how could he expand the business? How could he get new customers?

"That's simple. He hired me." Rolly smiled. "Bradley was not so much of a recluse at first, but he retreated more and more as time went on. Then he hired me as sales manager. That's my gift. We made a good team."

"And you stayed on after he left?"

"He sold me the business. A million down and ten thousand a month for ten years."

"Can the business support that?"

"Oh, sure. We clear well over twice that every month, on top of my salary. You always worry that some customers will leave when there is a transition, but we have managed to keep most of ours." Rolly smiled. "Of course, the new sales manager is not as good as I was."

"Then, it sounds as if you got a bargain."

"Sure. The building and equipment alone are worth more than two million. But I think Bradley was grateful to me for taking the selling off his hands. And he had been socking away the profits for a lot of years. I said he was a good strategist, and he invested his profits well. He became quite wealthy. You have to understand that Bradley was not a greedy man. He liked being successful, running a successful company. The money was proof of that, but he never cared that much about money."

"Did Bradley have any enemies? Disgruntled ex-employees? Competitors? Unhappy customers?"

Rolly looked at Devorkian keenly. "No, nothing like that. He took good care of his customers. And his employees. He was fair, and even generous. Of course, he didn't do all that himself. He hired a good HR specialist and good customer care reps. Some competitors were not happy that he was more successful than they were, but he did it all fairly and squarely. They couldn't really complain. He simply gave better service for a reasonable price." Rolly paused. "I think you have to interact with people to make enemies, don't you? Why did you ask if he had any enemies?"

Devorkian did not answer but continued asking questions. "Did you have any contact with Mr. Peterson after he moved to Winnipeg?"

"He sent me a change of address card, but I don't think it was an invitation to stay in touch. More the opposite. I think he was telling me he was moving away and not to contact him. Look, we worked together for twenty-five years, but we hardly ever talked face to face. I was out of the office a lot. We mostly communicated by email. Bradley preferred it that way. We weren't friends. We didn't hang out after work. I think he had a family, but I don't know for sure. He never talked about his personal life. I don't know what he did in his spare time."

Devorkian was silent for a few moments. "The thing is, we think it likely that Bradley Peterson was murdered. Can you think of anyone who would want to kill him?"

Rolly shook his head. "Wow. Murdered. That's a shock. That's nasty. I can't imagine anyone wanting to kill him."

"He was murdered in his condo about a year and a half ago," Devorkian continued. "He had no contact with anyone, and his body was only discovered a few days ago."

Rolly shook his head again. "No contact with anybody." He sighed. "That was Bradley. It's sad."

*****

The building's white stucco exterior was overlaid with streaks of dirty black and gray. There was an office at one end, and ten service bays stretched out away from it. A dozen trucks were in the parking lot in front. A large sign over the office door proclaimed in black block lettering: "WIN'S DIESEL."

Devorkian entered through the door. Behind a small counter was a man in a stained, gray T-shirt pulled tight around a bulging midriff and a "Win's Diesel" baseball cap.

209

He was in conversation with another man in a cleaner T-shirt and a Calgary Flames baseball cap.

"Help you?" The man behind the counter asked.

"Yes. I would like to talk to Markus Williams. I understand he works here," Devorkian said.

The man looked Devorkian over. "You a cop?"

"Yes."

"What's that bastard done now?" the man growled.

"Nothing, as far as I know," Devorkian said holding up his hands in a calming gesture. "I am not here to arrest him. I'm here to inform him about a death in the family."

The man behind the counter grunted and jerked his thumb. "Bay 7."

Devorkian nodded. "Thank you."

Devorkian walked back out the door and down the line to Bay 7. A man was leaning into the engine compartment of a semi.

"Markus Williams?" Devorkian inquired.

The man slowly pulled himself out of the engine compartment. Unruly black hair hung down to his shoulders below his greasy ball cap. His face was clean shaven but a deep brown streaked with black. "Yeah?" he said.

"I am Detective Devorkian from the Winnipeg Police."

"What you doing coming to my workplace? You trying to get me fired?"

"I am sorry to bother you at work, but I am only in town for a short time," Devorkian said evenly. "I have come to inform you that your father-in-law, Bradley Peterson, has passed away."

"Good riddance," Markus scoffed.

"You didn't like him?"

"Bastard was always breaking Angie's heart, making her cry. I kept telling her we didn't need him or his money."

"So, you wanted him dead?"

"I wanted him out of our lives."

"Then you will be glad to know that he was murdered. Did you have anything to do with that?"

"Hell, no! I been working. He moved away and good riddance! He's been gone a couple years. Why would I waste my time killing him?"

"Mr. Peterson was killed over a year and a half ago."

Markus shrugged. "Didn't know that. As I said, I been working. Ain't got no time to go kill somebody.

Devorkian nodded. "Thank you for your time."

Chapter 5

"How was your trip to Calgary?" Hosschuk asked.

"Informative but not very enlightening," Devorkain answered. "Bradley Peterson was almost as much a recluse there as he was here. I talked to his former wife, his son, his daughter, his son-in-law, and also the former sales manager who took over his business. They all said he was distant."

"Do you think one of them could have done it?"

Devorkian shook his head. "I just can't see it. You have to be angry with someone to commit murder, and mostly they seemed indifferent. The daughter was angry, but she was angry that he hadn't stayed in touch after he moved. She seemed surprised that he was dead. The son-in-law too. He disliked Peterson, and I've asked Calgary Police to check his alibi, but I don't expect that will go anywhere. This was a professional hit, and I don't think any of them would be capable of that. If the son-in-law had done it, he would have beaten Peterson to death and then trashed the condo."

"One of them could have hired a professional."

"I suppose," Davorkian said. "But they just don't seem the type." He paused. "How are things here?"

Hosschuk shrugged. "Nothing new from forensics yet. I'm going back to try to finish the door-to-door inquiries in the building." He paused. "But I did find out why he did not have any mail in his box. He gave the postal person a thousand dollars not to deliver unaddressed mail. He stopped paying her after he died, but she was afraid that if she started putting unaddressed mail in his box again, it would be found out that she had taken the bribe. By the way, I don't think I had noticed before, but the mailboxes all have the residents' names and unit numbers on them."

"The outside intercom just has unit numbers to protect the privacy of the residents, but anybody who succeeded in gaining access to the lobby could find any resident," Devorkian said. "Not very secure."

"Unbelievable," Hosschuk agreed.

*****

Another week had gone by. Devorkian was sitting quietly in his office staring at a handful of papers. Hosschuk knocked on the open door and walked in.

"You're not looking very cheerful," Hosschuk said.

"More forensic reports are in," Devorkian said. "They found no fingerprints other than the one set, presumably Peterson's, and no fibers or other evidence that could be from the killer."

"A professional hit."

"Yes, and the preliminary results from the autopsy show no alcohol in his system, but that doesn't mean anything because too much time has passed to make it detectable. Drug testing is not in yet but will likely show the same thing. Too much time has passed.

"A professional hit," Hosschuk repeated.

"Tell me what you have found," Devorkian said irritably. "Did you complete the door-to-door?"

"All but two units," Hosschuk said. "There's a Singh family on the fifth floor. The father's a dentist. The family has gone home to India for a visit, and they asked a neighbor to keep an eye on their place and pick up their mail. They're supposed to be gone for a month and won't be back for another week."

Devorkian frowned. "It's unlikely they'll have anything to contribute anyway."

212

"The other one is more likely," Hosschuk said. "A man named Brian Perry. He lives on the second floor, unit 221. The manager says he lives alone and he moved in about the same time as Peterson. He knows nothing else about him. I asked the neighbors on that floor, some people said they had seen him occasionally, but no one can remember when the last time was that they saw him, not for a couple of weeks at least."

"Interesting."

"Something else," Hosschuk continued. "A couple of residents said that Perry was not very social at first, avoiding contact, almost like Peterson, but that he became friendlier as time went on."

"That's how it is in an apartment building. There are no front porches or backyards to hang out in. You never see anybody, no one knows anybody, and you don't make friends."

"It's a condo complex," Hosschuk said.

"It's the same thing," Devorkian said dismissively. "Does he have a car?"

"Toyota Corolla, new model. I asked the manager to show me, and it's still in the underground parking."

"That's the best lead we have so far," Devorkian said.

"Any chance we could get a search warrant for his place?"

"No judge would grant that. There are not sufficient grounds," Devorkian said. "That service technician must have entered that unit. I wonder if he noticed anything."

"I thought of that and tracked him down. He says he serviced all the units, so he must have been in that one, but he doesn't remember seeing anything that stood out," Hosschuk said.

"See what you can find out about Perry," Devorkian instructed.

*****

"Devorkian."

"This is Constable Kuzmenko, on duty at the Toba Tower. I'm posted at unit 212, but I was also told to let you know if there is any activity at unit 221 down the hall. A man just went into that unit. He had a black shoulder bag, like a soft briefcase. He was carrying some papers and used a key."

"Right. Keep watching both units, and make sure the man does not leave. I'll be there in about fifteen minutes."

*****

"Devorkian."

"This is Constable Kuzmenko at the Toba Tower again. The man came out of unit 221. I asked him if he was Brian Perry. He said no. I asked him to identify himself, and I think he gave a fake name."

"Good. Keep him there. I'm about five minutes away."

*****

Devorkian strode down the hall toward unit 221, where Constable Kuzmenko was standing. Another, smaller man was standing behind him. As Devorkian approached, the smaller man stepped around the constable.

"Detective Devorkian!" the man said. "It's good to see you. This officer doesn't believe that I am—"

"John Smyth,' Devorkian said. "What are you doing here?"

"I came to check on my friend Brian's apartment."

Devorkian thought for a moment. "You have a key to Brian Perry's apartment? Would you mind opening the door and letting me have a look around?"

Smyth hesitated. "You don't have a warrant. Since Brian didn't give me permission, I can't give you permission."

"What are you afraid I'll find?"

214

Smyth was quiet for a moment. "I'm not afraid you will find anything incriminating, but there are rules against invasion of privacy and unjustified searches."

Devorkian sighed. "Okay. You'll have to come with me to the station."

"You know I don't carry a cell phone," Smyth said. "Could you call Ruby and let her know I'm being arrested again?"

"You're not being arrested. In fact, you've never been arrested, as far as I know. I just want you to make a statement."

"Okay, could you phone Ruby and tell her I'm being interrogated again?"

"You're not being interrogated! You're just providing some information that will help with our investigation."

"Your investigation of what?"

"We'll talk about it at the station."

*****

They were in a claustrophobic interview room at the main Winnipeg police station. Little had been said on the short ride in Devorkian's unmarked car. John Smyth was sitting on one side of the metal table, which was bolted to the floor. Devorkian was sitting across from him, with Sergeant Hosschuk off to one side taking notes.

"How do you know Brian Perry?" Devorkian began.

Smyth shrugged. "Brian's a pressman at Best Press, where we get *Grace* magazine printed. We met and became friends. Brian goes to our church and is in our care group."

Devorkian raised a quizzical eyebrow.

"Our care group has about eighteen people. We meet every week or two at our house to study the Bible, pray together, and care for each other..."

"I don't care." Devorkian interrupted. "What were you doing at Brian Perry's apartment?"

"He asked me to pick up his mail every few days, check on his place, and water the plants Audrey gave him."

215

"Who's Audrey?"

"Audrey Milner. She's also in the care group."

Devorkian sat up even straighter than usual. "What's her occupation?"

"She's an accountant. Why does it matter?"

"I'll ask the questions," Devorkian stated curtly. "Are Brian and Audrey romantically involved?"

"I think there's some mutual interest, but no, they're not dating. Why are you asking so many questions about Brian?"

"Because he's missing."

"I didn't know he was missing."

"Then where is he? Do you know?"

"His aunt is vey sick and probably dying. Brian went to take care of her. She's his only living relative."

"Where does she live? Where did Brian go?"

"I don't know. Possibly Calgary."

"Why Calgary?"

"That's where Brian said he used to live."

"And was he a pressman there too?"

"Yes, he said he worked for Fast Eddy's Printing."

Devorkian nodded.

"Why are you asking about Brian?" Smyth repeated.

"One of his neighbors died. We want to talk to everyone in the building to find out if they saw anything."

"The neighbor was murdered? Is that why there's a policeman stationed in the hall? I saw him there when I arrived."

Devorkian did not answer. "When did Brian leave?"

"He phoned me on the Friday a couple of weeks ago. I think he was leaving the next day."

"How was he getting to Calgary? Was he flying or driving?"

Smyth paused. "I don't know. I don't think he said."

"When is he coming back?"

"He said two or three weeks. I guess it depends on how the aunt is doing. She could die or get better or linger for a while. With old people, it's hard to say."

"Did he give you an address or contact information?"

"No, but I have his cell phone number. I guess he would take that with him."

"What is it?"

Smyth reached down for his shoulder bag, rummaged around in it, and came up with a dog-eared, black spiral book.

*****

John Smyth had been sent home in a police cruiser.

"By the time he picks up his car and gets home, he will be late for dinner," Hosschuk observed.

"That ought to give him something to have to explain to Ruby," Devorkian muttered.

Devorkian and Hosschuk were sitting in Devorkian's office.

"What do you think?" Hosschuk asked. "Could Perry be another victim?"

"What? The killer came back and killed another resident a year and a half later?"

"Maybe he was a witness?" Hosschuk suggested.

"If he was, the killer would have killed him right away or soon after. And if so, where's the body?" Devorkian said.

"Or do you think Perry's the killer and he went on the run?"

"I asked you to look into Perry. What did you find?" Devorkian asked.

"I checked social media, and he has no profile there. He moved into the Tower two years ago, but I can't find any record of him before that."

"So, he's using an alias?"

"Maybe. Do you think he could have moved into the Tower specifically so he could kill Peterson?"

"Or Peterson recognized who he was," Devorkian said. "But if he Killed Peterson, why would he run now?"

"He knew the inspection was coming up and the body would be discovered?"

217

"But he would have known the body would be discovered sometime, so why hang around for a year and a half? Leaving right when the body is discovered just makes him look guilty."

"Remember that some of the neighbors said he had become friendlier." Hosschuk suggested. How would that play in? Why would he change?"

"It doesn't fit in. You think he killed Peterson and then decided to treat the other residents better?"

"Maybe he relaxed once it became clear that the body would not be found for a while."

"Who knows why anyone would change?" Devorkian said. "It probably doesn't mean anything at all. He might not have become friendlier. Maybe it was the neighbors who became friendlier when they had become used to seeing Perry around. But Perry is still the best lead we have so far. If he didn't go away in his car, maybe he flew somewhere. Check airline passenger lists."

"Okay."

"There's something off about Perry," Devorkian mused. "He's disappeared, and we don't know where he has gone. And he knows Audrey Milner, Peterson's accountant. What are the odds of that?"

"Pretty slim, I would say. Accountants meet a lot of people, but it seems too much of a coincidence. But I just don't see how it fits together."

"Neither do I."

*****

"What have you found?" Devorkian asked

"There is no record of a Brian Perry flying to Calgary or anywhere else in the week before and the week after Peterson's body was found," Hosschuk reported.

"So, how could he have gone? By bus or rail? In that case, why not drive?"

"I don't know."

218

"I phoned the manager at Fast Eddy's Printing in Calgary," Devorkian said. "He's never heard of a Brian Perry."

"Suspicious."

"It certainly is. Keep looking."

Chapter 6

"Hi, John," Brian Perry said.

"Brian!" John answered. "Where are you?"

"I'm in a taxi coming back from the airport. I just got in."

"How's your grandmother?"

"Aunt."

"Yes, sorry. How's your aunt?"

"It's too soon to tell. The jury's still out on that. But the professionals have taken over. I'm not needed, at least for now."

"Okay," John said. "I should tell you that the police are looking for you."

"The police? Why?"

"A man down the hall from you was found murdered in his condo, and the police want to talk to everyone in the building. I think they found it suspicious that you went away just before the body was found and they couldn't contact you. I gave them your cell phone number."

"I had it turned off because I didn't think anyone from Winnipeg would need to contact me, and they were the only ones who had that number." Brian paused. "John, could you do me a big favor? Meet me at my place? Could you be there in ten minutes?"

"Ten minutes? I can do that, but it might take a little longer."

"Please try."

*****

John Smyth's old brown station wagon pulled into a visitor parking slot as Brian was getting out of the taxi. They met at the front entrance to the building.

"Thanks so much for coming," Brian said.

"No problem," John said.

They entered the building and rode up to the second floor in the elevator in silence. As they stepped out into the corridor, they could see two men standing in front of Brian's door.

Brian reached out and shook John's hand. "It's backwards," he said in a low voice. "If you don't hear from me in three hours, call this number." He continued more loudly. "Thanks, John. Would you put my suitcase into my condo for me?"

They approached the two men standing waiting at Brian's door.

"Detective Devorkian, how nice to see you again," John said. "This is my friend, Brian Perry."

*****

Brian Perry faced Devorkian and Hosschuk across a metal table in an interview room. The two policemen sat in silence for a full minute, but Brian did not flinch.

"Mr. Perry, do you know Bradley Peterson, who lives just down the hall from you?" Devorkian asked.

"Is he the man who was found dead in his condo?" Brian asked. "John told me."

"John Smyth talks too much," Devorkian said. "Now, answer the question. Do you know Bradley Peterson?"

"I don't know whether I would say I know him," Brian answered. "I've met him a couple of times."

"Tell me," Devorkian demanded.

"We met the first time on the day we moved in. We both happened to move in on the same day, the first Saturday in July two years ago. The manager was not happy about it because he said it tied up the elevator for too long. He said it was inconvenient and inconsiderate."

"You met Mr. Peterson?" Devorkian prompted.

"Yes, Mr. Peterson's moving van was already backed up by the front door. The main door was propped open, and Mr. Peterson was standing in the lobby next to Mr. Roberts, the manager. Mr. Roberts knew who I was because we had met when I bought my place, but he didn't seem happy to see me. He introduced me to Mr. Peterson and said that he was already moving in his stuff and I would have to wait to move mine in."

"What was your impression of Mr. Peterson?"

Brian thought a moment. "He seemed anxious, uncomfortable maybe. He didn't make eye contact. My impression was that he was shy and awkward."

"Did he say anything?"

"Not really. Sort of mumbled a hello. The movers started bringing in his furniture at that point, so he went off to supervise the furniture going into his condo. I explained to Mr. Roberts that I didn't have nearly as much furniture as Mr. Peterson, and he finally agreed that we could share the elevator. It helped that we were both only going to the second floor. Sometimes we both had boxes in the elevator at the same time."

"Did you see Mr. Peterson after that?" Devorkian asked.

"There was one thing. One of the movers got confused and brought a dolly of Mr. Peterson's boxes to my condo. They were all marked Fast Eddy's Printing in Calgary. I directed him back to the other condo, and I saw Mr. Peterson standing in the doorway. He sort of nodded to me but didn't say anything."

"John Smyth said that you had worked at Fast Eddy's yourself at some time. Is that right?" Devorkian asked.

Brian shook his head. "No, I never worked there. John must have misunderstood me. I never told him that."

"In my experience, Mr. Smyth gets a lot of things wrong. You said you met Mr. Peterson a couple of times," Devorkian pressed. "Are you talking about just that day?"

"No, I think I might have seen him in the hallway, and we talked maybe a couple of times, once in the elevator and once down in the lobby by the mailboxes."

"What did you talk about?"

"Nothing really," Brian said. "The weather? I don't remember. I got the impression that he would have liked to have a friend, but he hesitated. It was like he couldn't wait to get back to the safety of his condo. But that was only near the beginning. I haven't seen him for, I don't know, a long time."

"Think back to October the year before last," Devorkian said.

"Almost two years ago, you mean?" Brian asked.

"Yes. Do you remember seeing or hearing anything unusual about that time? Any visitors or workmen or strangers in the building?"

Brian let out a long breath and scratched his cheek. "October two years ago? Let's see. That would have been about when I started going to John's church. No, I don't remember anything from back then. It was a long time ago, and a lot has happened in the meantime."

"Where have you been?" Devorkian demanded suddenly.

"What? What do you mean?" Brian stammered.

"You've been away for over three weeks. Where were you?"

"Oh, that," Brian said. "I was away taking care of a sick aunt."

"Where?"

"Well, at her place."

"Where's that?" Devorkian demanded.

"Why do you want to know that? What difference does it make?" Brian said.

"Where were you?"

"I don't see how that's relevant."

"How did you get there? You didn't drive your car."

"I...I flew."

"No, you didn't. We checked the airlines. You weren't listed on any flight."

"I thought you wanted to know about Mr. Peterson. Why are you asking questions about me?"

"Because you have been off the grid for three weeks. Where were you?"

"You brought me here to ask about my neighbor, not pry into my private life."

"Why won't you answer the question?" Devorkian demanded. "What are you hiding?"

"I'm not hiding anything," Brian said. "But I know my rights. You have no right to ask me these questions. You have no grounds to suspect me of anything." He folded his arms and stared back at Devorkian.

*****

The voice on the other end of the line answered with an indecipherable grunt. It could have been "Yes," but John Smyth could not be sure.

"I'm calling on behalf of Brian Perry," John said. "I think he's been arrested."

"Why?"

"One of his neighbors was murdered some months ago. The police have been interviewing all the neighbors, and they took him to the police station to talk to him. Brian said if I didn't hear from him in three hours, I should call this number."

"Where?"

"He was arrested by Detective Devorkian, and I think they took him to the central police station in Winnipeg."

Before John could say anything more, the line went dead.

*****

Conrad Brown was six-foot-four and looked like a middle linebacker, big, powerful, and quick on his feet. His black, three-piece suit fit perfectly over his white shirt and black tie. He carried a black leather briefcase, and his dark hair was neatly trimmed and combed. He approached the front desk and spoke to the constable on duty.

"I'm here to see my client, Brian Perry," he said.

*****

"Who's he?"

Devorkian and Hosschuk were looking through the one-way glass at Conrad Brown and Brian Perry. The two men inside the interview room were standing with their back to the glass, so it was impossible to tell what they were saying. The larger man had a hand on Brian's shoulder.

"Name's Conrad Brown," Hosschuk answered.

"Is he with Brown and Sidney or Bond and Bond?" Devorkian asked.

"Don't know. He didn't give us a business card."

"Have you ever seen him before?"

"No. I know a lot of the lawyers in town, but not him."

Conrad Brown patted Brian on the shoulder, turned to the door, and knocked. A police officer opened the door.

Out in the corridor, Brown looked around and then approached Devorkian and Hosschuk. Devorkian carefully appraised him. It was not often that he encountered a man more elegantly dressed than he was.

"Conrad Brown," the man said with a smile.

"Detective Devorkian."

"Sergeant Hosschuk."

"You represent Mr. Perry?" Devorkian asked.

"You brought Mr. Perry in as a possible witness in the death of one of his neighbors," Brown said. "He has told you everything he knows about the victim. He was very forthcoming. Why is he still here?"

"Your client left town just before we found the body and stayed away for three weeks. And he won't tell us where he was."

"It is none of your business where he was," Brown said with another smile. "You have no right to ask him, and he doesn't have to tell you. He is a free citizen with a right to go where he wants without police permission."

"If he wasn't involved in the murder, why did he suddenly leave town?" Devorkian asked. "What was he doing?"

"He might have been going on a cruise. He might have been having an affair with a married woman. He might have been applying for a job. He might have been poaching lions in Africa or checking on his investments in Venezuela or spying for the Russians or committing a murder somewhere else. His private business is his private business. You have no reasonable grounds for suspecting him of any crime, and you have no right to hold him."

*****

"That was interesting," Devorkian said as Conrad Brown and Brian Perry walked to the outer door.

"Yes," Hosschuk replied. "But Brown was right. We had no grounds for holding him."

"What I'm wondering is how Brown knew Perry was here. Perry didn't make any phone calls."

*****

"It's always a pleasure seeing you Detective Devorkian,' John Smyth said.

Devorkian had breezed past Smyth's beautiful, blonde secretary Rachel, who stood behind him with a puzzled look on her face.

"It's okay, Rachel," Smyth said. "Detective Devorkian is an old friend." Turning to the detective, Smyth asked, "What can I do for you today?"

Devorkian moved into Smyth's office and sat in a worn chair across from the editor. "I have a question for you," he

225

said. "Yesterday, when you were with Brian Perry, did he ask you to make a phone call on his behalf?"

Smyth smiled. "Brian is my friend. He asked me to make a phone call, and I did. There is nothing wrong or illegal with that."

"Who did you call?"

"I don't know. Brian gave me the number on a piece of paper and said to make the call if I didn't hear from him in three hours."

"Do you still have the paper?"

"Sorry, no. I threw it away. I didn't think it was important to keep it."

Devorkian scowled, stood up, and left the office.

Chapter 7

"Where are we with the Peterson case?" Hosshuk asked a couple of months later.

"Right where we started, which is nowhere," Devorkian answered. "We finally got the DNA results, and the dead man is definitely Bradley Peterson, David Peterson's father."

"As we expected," Hoschuk said.

"Right, but we had to check," Devorkian said. "The Calgary police confirmed that Markus Williams was working the days we think Peterson was likely killed, and there is no record of any of the other family members coming here."

"I hate to say it, but I don't think we're going to solve this one. Is it time to pass it on to the Cold Case unit?"

"I don't like to do it, but I don't see what else we can do. We've checked everything we can think of, and we are out of leads."

"Do you still think Brian Perry could have done it?" Hosschuk asked.

"Possibly, but there's no evidence and no motive. I think he was up to something illegal but not this."

*****

226

"Thank you for seeing me," Conrad Brown said.

Devorkian looked over the well-dressed man sitting across from his desk. "You said you had information on the Bradley Peterson case?"

"Yes, I might be able to solve two cases for you, but first I would like to ask you a question. What is your assessment of this John Smyth character?"

"John Smyth? Why does he matter?"

"I have my reasons, which I may explain later. What about Smyth? Is he a good guy?"

"John Smyth is a religious fanatic and a pain in the backside, but he's mostly harmless."

"Mostly?"

"Well, he has a penchant for getting involved in police investigations."

"He's a criminal?"

"No, he's too religious and too commonplace for that. I think it's just that he knows people and gets so involved in the community that he keeps turning up like a bad penny. For instance, he knows two of the witnesses in the Bradley Peterson investigation. What are the odds of that? He's more intelligent than he seems and even bumbles into information that has been helpful in investigations on occasion."

"I see."

"You said you had information?" Devorkian pressed.

"Yes." Brown opened his briefcase and pulled out a file. He withdrew a photo from it and placed it on Devorkian's desk. "That's Ryan Scott."

It took Devorkian a few moments. "The unknown passenger on the flight that crashed. We have that photo."

"Do you have this photo?" Brown asked, placing another photo on the desk. The photo showed a man in a service uniform of some kind in a small lobby. "That's the same man entering the Toba Tower on October 9 two years ago."

"How did you get that?" Devorkian asked. "The manager said they only keep their security camera tapes for a month."

"We have been keeping an eye on the place," Brown said. "We have our own cameras."

Devorkian thought for a moment. "You're saying Ryan Scott flew into town to kill Bradley Peterson?"

"No, Ryan Scott flew into town to kill Bradley Peters, also known as Brian Perry."

"Wait a minute. You said 'we' were keeping an eye on the Toba Tower. Who are 'we'? You're not really Brian Perry's lawyer, are you?"

"I never said I was. I said Brian was my client. My law society credentials are beside the point." Brown pulled another photo out of the file folder and placed it on the desk. "That is Arven Krakowski, also known as Ryan Scott. He was an enforcer for the Yablonski crime gang in Toronto."

"He doesn't look quite the same…" Devorkian said.

"Cheek implants, a wig, and makeup," Brown said. "He's been known to use disguises in the past."

"Why would he come to kill Brian Perry?"

"Police in Toronto have been working to bring down the Yablonski crime gang for several years. Brian—Bradley Peters—was a key witness against that gang and has been in witness protection for over two years."

"Right. The key, unnamed mystery witness in the Yablonski gang trial," Devorkian said. "I've seen the news stories. But if you knew Ryan Scott was coming to kill Perry—Peters—why didn't you stop him?"

"Police have had the gang under intense surveillance for some time, including bugs and wiretaps, but the gang has been careful, and Krakowski is especially slippery. He changes addresses and phones regularly. We lost track of him. The first thing we heard was a cryptic message from him saying, 'Problem solved.' We immediately checked on Peters, and he was fine. It was only later that we picked up hints that Krakowski had died, maybe in a plane crash. Eventually, we connected him to Ryan Scott. We checked the surveillance tapes and found the photo I showed you. There's video. He stood at the front entrance checking his clipboard and looking at the intercom. Eventually, a resident came in. The resident unlocked the door and went in. At the same time, Krakowski pushed a button and said something into the intercom, probably something like, 'I'm here for your service call,' and 'Come on up.' He followed the other resident into the building before the door closed and ducked into the little alcove where the mailboxes are. Then, he went up in the elevator. We never saw him leave, so he must have gone out one of the exit doors from one of the stairwells."

"If you knew Krakowski had killed someone, why didn't you inform the Winnipeg police?" Devorkian demanded.

"By that time, it was several days later, no murders had been reported, and we weren't sure what to tell you. Was Krakowksi lying to the gang? Did he shoot at Peters or someone else and miss but thought he had succeeded? Besides, from our surveillance, we knew the gang thought Peters was dead, they wouldn't try to kill him again, and we didn't want you to raise their suspicions by launching an investigation into something that we weren't even sure had happened."

"So, you're thinking Krakowski killed the wrong man?" Devorkian asked. "You're saying he was a hit man for the gang. How could a professional make a mistake like that?"

"Criminals make mistakes all the time. You know that. We don't know how the gang found out Peters was in Winnipeg—that's another reason we didn't tell you about the hit, we didn't know where the leak was—so we're not sure exactly what information Krakowski had. Maybe he just knew the name of the building. And then there's the similarity of the names, Bradley Peters and Bradley Peterson."

"And Peterson was in 212 and Perry in 221," Devorkian said. "That's quite a coincidence."

"Coincidences do happen. And one other thing. We don't know a lot about Krakowski, but one thing we learned is that he was dyslexic. The gang had to give him directions in person."

"I don't normally believe in coincidences," Devorkian said, "but I guess it could happen."

"One thing puzzles me," Brown said. "How was it that Peterson's murder was not discovered for so long?"

"The Toba Tower is a very energy efficient and climate-controlled building. The body was in a bedroom which had its own thermostat. The killer—Krakowski, if it was him—turned the temperature down to just above freezing and left the fan running. The body essentially mummified. The killer also seems to have removed all perishable food from the unit so there would be no smell. And Peterson had arranged to have all his bills paid automatically, so there were no unpaid bills to trigger an investigation." Devorkian paused. "Do you think they will try again? I don't want another murder here. We can't guard Peters forever, and anyway it's not our job."

"It's unlikely. Since their first attempt failed, the gang probably isn't even sure where Peters is. Besides, Peters is no longer their biggest problem. The gang thought Peters was dead and there was a good chance they could get off. But when he showed up to testify, a couple of members of the gang panicked. They cut a deal. One of them, a man named Ivan Andrusyak, kept the books for the gang and turned them over. That not only solidified the current cases but also allowed investigators to lay more charges and identify a few more gang members. The gang is too busy turning on each other to worry about Peters."

"In all of that information, is there enough evidence to convict those responsible for Bradley Peterson's murder?"

"I wouldn't think so. We know from wiretaps that Yablonski ordered Krakowski to kill Peters, but Krakowski did not kill Peters. Our video places Krakowski in the Toba Tower, although that could be questioned by a good defence team. The video does not place him in Peterson's unit, and Krakowski is dead and cannot be questioned. I think you will have to call it a SNOT."

"A snot?"

"Solved but NO Trial."

Devorkian shook his head. "We call it Closed Without Conviction."

"It doesn't matter. We have far better evidence on a long list of crimes. Those responsible for Peterson's death are heading to prison, most of them for life."

*****

The early evening sun was pouring into the Smyths' living room, shining light on the assembled faces of the care group.

"Before we get started tonight, Brian has something he would like to say," John said.

Brian took a deep breath. "I can't tell you what a great blessing it has been to be in this group," he said. "You've made me feel so welcome. That's why it's so hard for me to tell you that I haven't been completely honest with you. For one thing, my real name is Brad Peters, not Brian Perry."

"That's good to hear," Audrey said. "I never liked the name Brian."

Brian paused and then moved on. "I am in witness protection."

"Duh," Dan Miller said. "Tell us something we didn't know."

"You knew?" Brian asked."

"It was pretty obvious," Reuben said. "We didn't really know, but we suspected it was something like that. You told us nothing about your background or past life. It was clear you were hiding something. You seemed uneasy, like you were always looking over your shoulder. Witness protection was a good guess."

"We talked about it, and that was the general consensus," Angelo Moscatelli added. "You said you had no family, and yet you went away to take care of a sick aunt."

"I'm sorry," Brian said. "It was the best thing I could think of at the time. I'm not very good at making things up

231

on the spot. Another man moved into the building the same day I did, and he had boxes marked Fast Eddy's Printing in Calgary. I worked at a print shop, so I told John that I worked there. It was in the opposite direction to Toronto where I had really lived. But then John said he knew someone who worked there, and that really threw me. After that, I decided it was safer to just not say anything."

"I made that up," John said. "I don't know anybody who worked at that shop. I thought you were telling me a story, and I wanted to test if that was the case."

"You knew I was lying, and you still invited me to your house?" Brian said.

"What I knew was that you needed a friend," John said.

Brian took a deep breath. "My parents died in a car crash when I was twenty. So, that part was true. I really do have no family, other than some distant cousins I wasn't in touch with anyway. I was left on my own. My parents owned a house and some investments, as well as life insurance. So, I had money, but no guidance. I had already enrolled in a graphic arts program. After I graduated, I got a job at a company called Yabor Printing. It was a pretty big company. I ran a press and also did some design work—book covers, restaurant menus, advertising brochures, that kind of thing. It was okay, I made decent money, but it wasn't very fulfilling. What I didn't know is that the shop was owned by the Yablonski crime family. One day, I was asked to come back in the evening to work on a special project. I was told I would be designing passports and other identification for use in a movie production. That was more challenging and fun. They also told me to design fake IDs for high school students to get into bars. I did a few, I felt a little uncomfortable with that, but it wasn't a big deal. I said something about it to the manager, a man named Ivan Andrusyak. That's when he took me aside and said that I was the one who had signed off on all the paperwork for the things I had been designing. They hadn't gone through the company books. If there was ever an investigation, I would be the one who would take the blame. The company would say I must have been doing the work on my own after hours. Andrusyak also told me that they now owned me and I would have to do whatever they said. If I didn't like it, I would not like what they would do to me. The work really ramped up after that. As I said, I was a good graphic designer. But I began saving copies of what I was designing on my phone. I was being paid well, but it was pretty dicey. Then, one day, I was told to design a passport and other documents for a certain man. I did, but two days later, I saw on the news a photo of the man whose documents I had designed. He had killed his wife and children and had already left the country using the documents I had made. I knew I couldn't continue. That's when I went to the police and told them what I had been doing. I gave them a copy of all of the documents I had been designing. I kept working for a couple of weeks, and the police made me wear a wire, a listening device. It was terrifying. Somehow the gang became suspicious, and the cops pulled me out and got me to Winnipeg. Among the last things I had designed were fake documents for me. As I said, I had money, so I bought the condo in Toba Tower."

The others sat in silence, letting this sink in.

"And when you went away to take care of a sick aunt?" John prompted.

"I was testifying at a trial for some of the gang members," Brian said.

"That must have been terrifying," Audrey said.

"We were praying for you," John said. "We prayed that it would go well."

"And that you would be kept safe," Audrey added.

Brian took a deep breath. "Thank you for that. It was terrifying, even worse than I expected. I didn't fly there on a regular flight. The police flew me in on one of their planes and put me up in a hotel under a different name. When I got there, the police told me that the gang was surprised to find out that I would be testifying because they thought they had killed me a couple of years before. That really shook me."

"Are you still in danger? Are they going to try again to kill you?" Audrey asked.

"That's a strange thing. The police think I should stay in witness protection just to be sure, but they think I should be okay. As I said, the gang didn't expect me to testify, and they were hoping they would get off. But when I showed up, some of them decided they needed to make a deal. One of them was Ivan Andrusyak, and he had a lot more evidence against the gang than I did. It is now more likely that the gang members will be convicted, some of them already have been, and if any of them are still out of jail and want to go after someone, they will likely go after him rather than me."

"We were praying," John said. "That sounds like an answer to prayer to me."

"Why did they think you were dead?" Dan asked.

"They had sent someone to kill me," Brian said, "but they killed the wrong man."

"Bradley Peterson," Audrey said. "I did his accounting for him. He died in October last year, but they didn't find his body until recently. It was really sad. He apparently had no friends or family, and no one missed him."

"He lived on my floor. He moved in the same day I did. I was about to have my stuff unloaded and there was another truck backed up to the front door. I approached the manager, and he introduced me to the other man. He said, 'This is Bradley Peterson.' That threw me. I thought he was talking about me for a second. Then I didn't know what to think. I didn't know whether the police had moved him in to keep an eye on me or if he was part of the gang. He's the one who had some boxes marked Fast Eddy's Printing in Calgary, and I didn't know whether that was a clue from the police that I should say I was from Calgary. But, after a while, I decided the whole thing was just one of those strange coincidences."

"Maybe one of God's coincidences," Angelo suggested.

"Or maybe one of the devil's. His name was similar to my real name, and I guess that's why they killed him by mistake. I met him a couple of times after that, but he didn't seem like he wanted to talk to me. But, to tell the truth, I didn't try very hard to talk to him either."

"You were afraid of him and worried that he might be part of the gang?" John suggested.

"Not by then. The thing is, I was just as much a loner as he was."

"The whole thing is creepy," Audrey said quietly.

"And all the time he was lying dead in the Toba Tower just down the hall from me," Brian said. "It's disturbing that he died in my place. It should have been me."

"Just like Jesus died in your place for your sins," John suggested.

"Yes, except that Jesus did it on purpose and Bradley Peterson had no choice in the matter. He never agreed to die for me." Brian paused. "And the strangest thing is that he died near the beginning of October two years ago. That's just about the time that John first invited me to the men's group and then I started going to church and I met all of you. It could have been him who was invited to church and me who had his life. It's not just that he got the death that was meant for me, but I could have had the life that he had—no friends, no family, and no purpose. I would have had that. That's where I was headed. I was alone."

"God places the lonely in families," John said.

"Yes! That's what He did for me. It frightens me the way I was. When the Yablonski crime family threatened me, they didn't say, 'We're going to kill you.' They said, 'You're a dead man.' And I was—a walking, talking, breathing dead man."